CANCELLED

NEMESIS

THE BEAST WITHIN

CATHERINE MACPHAIL

NEMESIS
THE BEAST WITHIN

BLOOMSBURY

First published in Great Britain in 2007 by Bloomsbury Publishing Plc
36 Soho Square, London, W1D 3QY

A CIP catalogue record of this book is available from the British Library

ISBN 978 0 7475 8269 4

All papers used by Bloomsbury Publishing are natural, recyclable products made
from wood grown in well-managed forests. The manufacturing processes conform
to the environmental regulations of the country of origin.

Typeset by Dorchester Typesetting Group Ltd
Printed in Great Britain by Clays Ltd, St Ives Plc

1 3 5 7 9 10 8 6 4 2

www.macphailbooks.com
www.bloomsbury.com

For Robert and Ross

The ice-cold March winds rattled through my clothes. I pulled my coat tighter about me, glad of it on the moors tonight. Suddenly, the full moon shot out of the clouds and just ahead a clump of tall pine trees seemed to come alive. I could see them silhouetted against the midnight sky as they swayed and rustled in the wind. Should I be afraid? I bet lots of boys my age would be, out here on the moors at midnight. Alone. Yet, after all I'd come through in the last few days, I was sure I would never be afraid again.

I was afraid of nothing.

I picked up my pace, heading towards the trees. There would be shelter for me for the night under one of those swaying trees maybe. And after that, where was I going? All I knew was that I had to search out my past, find the secret locked inside me before the Dark Man found me again. And he would. No doubt about that.

Was I afraid of him? I'd be stupid not to be. But I'd beaten him once, and I was cocky enough to believe I could beat him again.

As soon as I stepped into the wood it was as if the trees ate me up. The sky disappeared. I was surrounded by the pitch dark. All I could hear was the wind whistling through the tall trees. I could see nothing.

I strode on, too sure of myself – I knew that a split second later when I heard a sound, a low growl that came from somewhere between the trees. I twirled round, expecting to see someone there, watching me. I peered through the dark. Nothing . . . but I couldn't be certain. I couldn't trust my own eyes. Did I see a movement, a dark shape shifting silently somewhere close by?

Then, that sound again; an ominous growl, closer this time.

A fox, I thought. There was a fox there in the trees. I turned my back on it and kept walking. I wanted it to know I was no threat. I wasn't a threat to him, and he was no threat to me. It was only a fox out hunting for food for his family.

I'm not your food, I almost shouted back to him, but I stayed silent, walked on.

The thought leapt at me. Did foxes growl?

They must, I assured myself.

On cue, the growl came again. Even closer behind me, as if whatever it was – a fox? – had padded silently after me. Too close. I had to see, almost stumbled as I turned my head to look back.

The dark shape seemed to be moulded into the pines. But I could see it moving. No mistake this time. And I knew now it wasn't a fox. Too big for a fox. That growl too menacing.

Were those eyes I could see, pinpoints of green light, watching me?

Suddenly, all I wanted was away. Afraid of nothing!

What a load of rubbish. I was afraid now. Afraid to run. Afraid not to.

Something told me I should stay as still as a shadow, make it believe I was dead. Not move a single muscle.

The growl, so loud this time, made my bones quiver. With a liquid movement the shape took a step towards me, closing in.

I couldn't have stayed still if you'd paid me. Instinct took over. I began to run.

I could hear it behind me, a soft pounding. One leap and it would surely be on me. Fear gave me speed. I broke out of the trees on to the open road, half hoping it wouldn't follow. Some hope. Still it came after me, so close I could hear the slavering of its jaws. I could never run fast enough to get away from this – whatever 'this' was. I didn't dare risking a look to find out.

And there was nowhere to hide. No escape.

All I knew was that something was after me, and it wanted me dead.

1

SUNDAY, MIDNIGHT

Was this how I was going to die? Eaten by something hungry on dark moorland? It was still after me, closer and closer it came; I could hear it pounding at my heels. Could I feel the hot breath on my neck, or was that just my terrified imagination? I couldn't run any faster, wanted desperately to look back, didn't dare.

Suddenly, I was blinded by light.

It was a car, there on the moonlit road, racing towards me. My mind was crazy for survival. I held my hands high in the air. Still running, never stopping running. I waved my arms wildly for it to stop.

'Help!' I screamed the word out.

I saw nothing beyond the headlights. Rescue was all I could think of. I ran towards the lights, wasn't going to stop till I was safe. I didn't even care if the car hit me. There was something after me and I wanted away from it.

The car slowed as it approached. The front door swung open. I kept running, sure I could still hear the pounding of paws almost on me. I saw a hand reach out from the car. I kept running, stretched out, grabbed it.

Felt human skin. I was never more glad to feel the touch of a human hand. I gripped the hand – a firm hand – held on, felt myself being hauled inside the car.

I landed on the floor, my legs still hanging outside – imagined it, whatever 'it' was, snapping at my ankles, biting off my feet, leaving me with only bloody stumps. The thought almost made me faint. I felt as if I was slipping into unconsciousness.

'Get your feet inside! Close the door!'

The command brought me to my senses. I drew my legs in, leant across and yanked the door shut. The car revved up and sped off. I was breathless, lay still on the floor of the car. Did I hear howling? I imagined that I did.

At last, I looked up. The man who was driving, my rescuer, had a mane of dark golden hair, a strong straight nose. His face was grim, and the hands that gripped the steering wheel were flecked with freckles.

At last I found the breath to speak. 'Thanks.'

'What the hell are you doing out on the moors?' He seemed angry at me. 'Everyone knows there's something out there.' He glanced at me. His eyes were a piercing blue.

I tried to think of a sensible answer. Why was I out here? Somehow I didn't think I could tell him the truth.

Haven't a blinking clue. That was the truth. Don't know who I am. Or where I came from. No memory, until I woke up a couple of weeks ago in the stairwell of a tower block, and since then I've been a murder suspect, almost killed not once but four times, and I'm being chased by a Dark Man who seems to think I have some kind of terrible secret locked in my memory. Didn't even have a name, just one I had made up from nowhere.

Ram.

I licked my lips, hoping he might think my hesitation was nerves, and not me desperately trying to think up a story he might just believe.

I pulled myself up on to the seat and looked behind me into the pitch darkness. Even the moon had gone behind a cloud. There was nothing to be seen on the long black road.

Had it really happened? It seemed now as if I had only been in some kind of a nightmare.

The man asked again. 'What are you doing here?'

I'd had time to think. 'I lost my group,' I said at once. 'School trip, you know.'

That only made him angry. 'People will be looking for you! I wonder if there's any mention of you on the local radio station.' He leant across to switch on the car radio.

I stopped him. 'It's OK. My teacher knows where I am. I'm meeting up with him.'

'Where's your mobile?' he asked. 'Call him. Let him know you're safe.'

That was the last thing I wanted, anyone looking for me. 'I've already called him, told him I'd meet up with him tomorrow. No mobile . . .' I patted my pockets. 'Must have lost it, running.'

It sounded weak and implausible, even to me. Must have sounded more so to him. 'Well, your teacher should be fired, leaving a boy on the moors, on his own. There's a dangerous swamp on those moors and there's supposed to be something out there. Some kind of beast. It's been in all the papers.'

'It was chasing me.' I heard again in my imagination the low growl, the sound of paws pounding behind me. 'Didn't you see it?'

The man shook his head. 'Only saw you. Running for your life.' He turned back to the road ahead. 'I'm taking you back to my house. My wife and I live in a cottage up the road. Shouldn't be doing it, but I haven't any choice. You can call somebody from there.'

Think fast, Ram, I thought. *How can I explain everything so he'll believe it? How am I going to get myself out of this one?*

The man looked back at me and smiled. He took his hand from the wheel and touched my shoulder gently. 'My wife's at home. Don't worry. We'll get everything sorted out.'

I leant back in my seat. We were in the middle of nowhere. Blackness all around me. I had a sudden urge, might even have been a premonition, to leap from the car. Take my chances with whatever kind of beast was out there.

Too bad I didn't.

2

I saw the welcoming lights of a cottage far in the distance, the only sign of civilisation. 'That's home,' the man said.

'Bit remote,' I said.

'We like it that way,' he answered.

Every instinct I had warned me this was a bad idea. A boy should not be going back to the house of a stranger. But then, I was not your normal boy in a normal situation. I was taking chances every day, just to stay alive.

'Hungry?' he asked me as he turned off the one-track road on to the bumpy path that led to his cottage. 'My wife's a great cook. She'll have something hot ready.'

A hot meal – sounded good. Too good to miss. I got out of the car and followed him into the house.

'Mary!' he called out as soon as he opened the door, and a woman appeared almost at once. She had dark curly hair and a sweet face. I suppose some people might have called her pretty.

'William!' She smiled at the man, then her eyes darted to me. 'Well, hello?'

The man, William, was taking off his coat and hanging it on a hook by the door. 'Found him running up on the moors. He said that thing, whatever it is, was after him.'

She gasped, stared at me. 'Did you see it? I thought it was just a rumour. Didn't think it really existed . . . No one's actually seen it yet. There have just been lots of stories.'

I might have told her then what little I had seen, if the man, William, hadn't interrupted her. 'If he spotted it, maybe we should get the police in – let them know.'

That decided me. I shook my head. The last thing I wanted was the police involved. 'Didn't really see anything. I was just so scared. Might have been my imagination. The dark getting to me.'

The man looked at me, puzzled. 'Well, you were running as if the devil himself was after you.'

I said nothing. Still he watched me. 'Are you sure you're all right?' he asked.

I didn't get a chance to answer. Just as well – I had no answer.

The woman, Mary, came hurrying down the hallway towards me. 'Goodness, William, stop asking the boy questions. It's late and it's too cold to think straight. He can explain everything in the morning.' She smiled at me. 'Are you hungry?'

I nodded. The smell of food was wafting from the kitchen. I felt my mouth water, heard my stomach rumble. She heard it too. She laughed, helped me off with my coat. Jake's coat. I didn't want to part with it. Had no choice. She held it out to William and he took it from her.

'Go on,' he said to me. 'Go and eat.'

And Mary led me into the kitchen.

William waited until the kitchen door was safely closed before he hung the boy's coat on a hook. Then, slowly, he put his hand in each pocket. Nothing. The pockets were empty.

The boy had nothing on him. No rucksack. No mobile phone. No identification of any kind. And a very implausible story. A lie – he was sure of it.

And William smiled.

3

I ate like an animal, finishing off a huge plate of stew in no time. Then I wiped the gravy from the plate with thick slabs of bread. Mary sat beside me, watching me.

'My goodness, you were hungry.'

I drew my hand across my mouth. 'That was great, thanks.'

She lifted the plate from the table, still smiling. There was something about that smile that gave me the creeps. Maybe I just wasn't used to people smiling at me.

William came in then. He was smiling too. 'I've made the bed up in the spare room for you.'

I was already shaking my head. 'No. no. You've done enough for me. I'll just get going.'

'You can't go anywhere at this time of night. Tomorrow I'll take you wherever you want to go. But for now . . . I think you should phone your teacher. I'd say phone home, but that might just freak your parents out. Lost out here on the moors with a couple of strangers. Let your teacher know exactly where you are and who you're with. I'll talk to him too, make sure he knows our number. This isn't something we would normally do either, so I want him to know you're in safe hands.'

'We've no choice, William. We can't send him out into the night alone,' Mary said quickly.

I was trying to think fast. Could I tell them I couldn't remember the teacher's number? Or that my parents were off on a much-needed holiday? No. Maybe then they really would contact the police.

Anyway, if they were so keen for me to call someone, give them the exact location of their house, even their phone number, then surely they had no sinister motives behind helping me. They were just what they appeared to be. Good people who smiled a lot.

'I'll phone the teacher,' I said suddenly.

'Good,' William said. 'Although it's a good telling-off he needs.'

Last thing I needed was for William to want to lecture this fantasy teacher of mine.

I dialled a series of numbers, hoped it might just reach someone, but even so I would talk to dead air if it didn't.

'It's ringing,' I said. And it was.

William and Mary watched me. She was washing the dishes, he was drying them.

I was just about to pretend to leave a message when the phone was answered by a sleepy voice. 'Who the bloody hell is phoning me at this time in the morning?'

'It's Ram,' I said, saying my name without even thinking. 'It's just to let you know I'm safe and well . . .'

The blurry voice on the phone was annoyed. 'Who the hell is Ram?'

'I know, sir, it was my fault. I got lost, Mr . . .' I looked

9

round desperately for a name for this imaginary teacher of mine, saw one on a picture hanging on the wall. 'Mr Vettriano.'

'Are you winding me up, son?' The voice didn't sound sleepy any longer, now he was getting angry.

'I'm here at . . .' I looked at William.

'Red Berry Cottage,' he said, then followed it up with a name and an address, postcode and all. Mr Vettriano had started swearing at this point.

'Give him our phone number too,' William told me. I repeated it down the line as William told it to me.

He put down the dishtowel, came towards me, holding out his hand. 'Here . . . let me talk to him.'

I swallowed, looked blank probably. Or just guilty. I held out the phone. 'Aw, got cut off.' I pushed buttons furiously. 'Bad signal, I think.'

'You want to call him again?'

I shook my head. 'He's raging. He's going to kill me, he says . . . That's our Mr Vettriano. You don't mess with him.'

'I should have spoken to him,' William said. 'Never mind. He has our number. He can phone back any time.'

🏃

The man was still swearing and talking to himself angrily. 'Mr Vettri . . . what! What kind of name is that? And having the cheek to phone me! Calling me a name like that!'

His wife had dumped him a long time ago. He had no one else to talk to. 'And at this time in the morning.' It was a boy winding him up, he was sure of it. The boys around here were always winding him up. Rapping at his door and running away. Shoving things through his letterbox. Scrawling graffiti on his walls. He was sober enough to press the last-caller button.

'The caller has withheld their number,' the disembodied voice told him.

'Typical!' he yelled into thin air. 'That's it! My phone's going off the hook for the rest o' the night!'

4

Mary showed me the room I was to sleep in. There was a single bed by the window, made up with a scarlet fluffy duvet. There were posters on the wall, motorbikes and racing cars – even the lamp on the bedside table was the headlights of a car. This was a boy's room, but where was the boy?

She took a pair of pyjamas from a drawer and laid them on the bed. 'You'll be ready for anything after a good night's sleep,' she said. 'Now drink up your hot chocolate.'

She'd even made a nightcap for me.

At the door, she turned to me and smiled. 'There's a lock on this door if it makes you feel safer. OK?'

They couldn't have any sinister intentions. Now I was sure of it. A lock on the door to make me feel safe? Insisting I contact my teacher? Offering to take me to a police station? Even making me a nightcap. No. I had a feeling I had figured out what I had stumbled upon. They had lost a son, a boy my age, kept his room exactly the way he had left it. Creepy, but I was sure it must happen a lot.

Yes, I had simply landed lucky this time.

Why could I never just accept good luck?

Too good to be true . . . that was the phrase that kept repeating itself inside my head.

Good food, a warm bed, safety. Even a pile of books by the bedside table. *Treasure Island, The Twits, Hansel and Gretel*.

I wouldn't sleep, of course, I promised myself. I'd just rest my eyes. I'd lock the door, lie on the bed and rest my eyes.

And in the middle of the night, when they were both fast asleep, I'd go.

'Have you phoned the number?' Mary asked when she came downstairs.

William nodded. 'Engaged. Probably off the hook. Definitely not a mobile phone, and not a concerned teacher.'

Mary smiled. 'And nothing in his pockets?'

'Not a thing.'

'Could we really be so lucky?'

'And why not?' William smiled back at her. 'The boy's on the run – doesn't want to be found. I think he's the one for us.'

It was at that moment they heard the howl, somewhere out on the dark moors.

And they smiled again.

I had almost drifted off to sleep when I heard it. It jerked me awake, that eerie sound. I leapt to my feet and crossed to the window.

All was blackness. Total blackness.

But somewhere out there, was the Beast.

5

MONDAY

It was the smell of bacon that woke me. Wafting up the stairs, deliciously filling my nostrils, dragging me from a deep, heavy sleep. I opened my eyes, and for a moment, a wonderful moment, I thought I was home. Breakfast was being cooked by my mother, in the kitchen. My dad was revving the car up outside.

Then I remembered. I had no home, no real memory of one. Why couldn't I remember? What had happened to make me forget?

I was warm in the bed. I was cosy, warm – such a wonderful feeling. Who knew where I would sleep tonight? Who knew when I would ever be warm again? I'd kept my clothes on, planning to make a speedy getaway in the night. That had been all forgotten; I had slept so soundly.

And now the smell of that bacon was making me hungry, and hunger won over comfort. I slipped from the bed and crossed to the window. The man, William, was closing the doors of the old wooden garage. His car, a battered old silver one, sat outside on the driveway. He looked up at me, as if he sensed I was there, watching him. He smiled and waved. I waved back, even managed a smile too. They were all right, I had decided, this William and Mary. Good people. Why had I suspected anything funny about them? I had had a good night's sleep. The world looked bright and hopeful this morning.

I dragged the chest of drawers from the locked door (well, I wasn't taking any chances last night), and I went out on to the landing. Mary appeared at the bottom of the stairs. She smiled up at me. I just wished they wouldn't smile quite so much.

'Good morning. Sleep OK?'

I nodded. 'Like a baby,' I said.

'Slept in your clothes, I see.'

'So tired.' I hoped she didn't see me blush. 'Just flopped on the bed and I was away into dreamland.'

I was lying – could she tell that?

'I've left some fresh clothes for you on the chair beside your room.' I turned, and sure enough, there was a pile of clothes, neatly folded. Trousers, a shirt, a sweater. I remembered the son I was sure they once had and I shivered. Was I expected to wear a dead boy's clothes?

'Have a shower,' she called again and pointed to a door. The bathroom obviously. 'Then come down and have some breakfast.'

I could smell coffee now too. Freshly brewed coffee. I lifted the clothes from the chair. They smelt fresh and clean. So what if they had once belonged to their son? He didn't need them now. And I did.

It was only the hunger that stopped me from lingering

16

longer in the shower. When I was finished I wiped the steam from the mirror and looked at myself. My mop of dark hair, still with hints of red dye in it, was clean for a change, my face shiny. Who did I look like, with my dark brown eyes and my sallow skin? Who was I?

One day, I would find out. I had to keep believing that. Until then I had to keep out of the clutches of the Dark Man.

The bacon was sizzling as I walked into the kitchen. 'These clothes are a great fit.' Mary didn't say anything. She only put a plate of eggs, bacon and sausages in front of me. I was suddenly sorry I had said that. Last night I was sure I had figured out the truth about them. They had a lost a son, a boy my age. These were his clothes. How kind of them to let me wear them.

'This is really good of you,' I prattled on. 'The food, the bed. I really appreciate it. I'll be on my way as soon as I've eaten.'

'Coffee or tea?' she asked.

'Coffee,' I said. 'I can't resist that smell.' She was being so kind I wondered if I had the nerve to ask her to make up some sandwiches for me before I left.

William came in just as I was wiping up egg yolk with a thick slice of bread.

'Ready to go?' he said.

Fed and rested, I was ready for anything. 'Any time you are,' I said. 'But you don't have to give me a lift.'

He shook his head and tutted. 'Nonsense. You can't walk. Can't have you late for your first day at your new school, Noel.'

6

I almost choked on my crispy bacon. 'Who's Noel?' I asked.

William and Mary glanced at each other. He raised an eyebrow. 'Why, you are.'

I shot to my feet. 'What?!'

William sighed. 'Come on, Noel. Joke's over. You should have started school two weeks ago. You can't put it off any longer.'

I was looking for somewhere to run, but he was blocking my escape route to the door. 'I'm not this Noel. I'm . . .' and I hesitated. Because, who was I? 'I'm not this Noel,' was all I could say again.

'Please don't cause any more trouble, Noel. Uncle William and I have put up with enough.'

Uncle William! Suddenly, they were related to me! 'You trying to tell me you're my uncle?'

He was nodding. 'I'm Uncle William and this is Aunt Mary, as if you didn't know.'

What was happening? I was afraid. 'I don't know who you are, but you are not my aunt and uncle.'

He stood straight, looked angry. 'Who are we, then?'

'I don't know. You picked me up on the moors last night.'

He didn't disagree with that. 'Yes. You'd run away again.'

The woman spoke. 'So if you aren't our Noel . . . who are you?'

I couldn't answer that. Didn't know who I was, did I? 'My mum will be looking for me. I have to go,' was all I said.

'Call her.' Mary even lifted the phone, held the receiver out to me.

And I was lost then. I had no mother. I had no one to phone.

William threw a jacket towards me. 'Here. Put this on. It's cold out there.'

I caught the jacket. A bright red jacket. But not mine. 'This isn't my jacket.' I wanted my coat – the one Jake had given me. I wanted something I could recognise. Something that at least had a bit of my past in it. Something reassuring.

'Put it on,' was all he said. 'It's cold. Come on. We have to get to school.'

I decided it was better if I got out of the house. I could escape then. Jump from the car if I had to. Run.

The jacket fitted me too. It could have been made for me. The woman, Mary, hugged me at the door. My arms fell limp at my side, but I let her hug me. 'Have a good day, Noel.'

'I'm not Noel!' I snapped it out. They were making me afraid. All of this was making me afraid.

I couldn't run as we walked to the car. William held

19

my arm tightly. I was like a zombie, staring straight ahead, trying to think. The woman still stood at the door, watching.

'Aren't you going to wave to your aunt?'

'She's not my aunt,' I said again.

As the car turned on to the road, it almost slowed to a halt. I took my chance. I snapped at the handle, pulled it. Nothing happened. The door stayed shut.

'Child lock,' the man said. His eyes never left the road. 'You've tried that one many times before.'

I sat back in the seat, trembling – caught sight of my reflection in the car window. I could see the fear there. But more than fear. The face that stared back at me was confused and frightened. But there was something else. Something worse than fear. Because I couldn't be sure – sure that just maybe they were telling me the truth.

Was this really my life? Was I really this Noel?

7

I watched the barren landscape flit by, the moss frosted white, the tips of the mountains hidden by cloud, fog creeping down from the jagged summits to settle on the ground below.

This couldn't be happening. Who were these crazy people? I was not this Noel. I kept repeating that to myself.

Yet . . . who was I, then?

I had a memory that only stretched back, not months, hardly weeks, but days. I had awoken in a tower block and been caught up in a murder, an explosion and death. But before that . . . nothing.

And what reason would they have for lying? What would be the point of pretending I was their nephew, Noel? It didn't make sense. The clothes fitted me. He was taking me to a school I should have started at two weeks ago, but I had run away, two weeks ago. And I had no memory of anything before two weeks ago.

The clothes weren't the only things that fitted. It all did.

'So why didn't you tell me I was this Noel last night? You even let me phone my teacher,' I asked him.

'We've learnt it's wiser to go along with you when you're like that. You're usually better in the morning.'

I turned on him then. 'What do you mean, I'm usually better in the morning?!'

'You always come back with some story. You don't know who you are. You can't remember what happened. The psychiatrist said we –'

I couldn't even let him finish that one. 'The psychiatrist . . . now I have a psychiatrist?!'

'Psychologist . . . a child psychologist.' He turned to me then and his face was full of concern . . . At least, that was the way it looked. Concern. 'It's not your fault, Noel. Over the past months you've had a lot to deal with. It's because of everything that's happened to you that you're like this.'

I wanted to ask him what had happened to me. My insides were trembling like the beginnings of an earthquake, and I was frightened.

When we reached the school I would make my decision. I could run then, or perhaps stay around and find out more.

The school was a one-storey brick-built building that looked as if it had once been a farmhouse. There was a covered walkway leading from the back to some kind of shed. The schoolhouse itself seemed to be on the edge of nowhere, hemmed in by the cloud-tipped hills. Halfway down the dirt road leading to the school the driveway split in two and one of the paths turned towards a house a little way beyond the school itself. Two-storey grey stone with the windows painted a bright red. As if someone was trying hard to make it a home.

The man, this Uncle William, checked his watch. 'We're a bit late. But I want to have a chat with the teacher anyway.' He looked at me. 'His name's Mr Darling.' He smiled. Said what I was thinking. 'Bet he gets the mickey taken out of him about that.'

I didn't smile back. I was too confused.

He stopped the car, and had to come round to my side to open the passenger door. Then he stood close to me as we walked towards the front door of the school, as if he knew first chance I got I'd run off again.

Mr Darling saw them arrive. The old silver car pulled to a halt close to the front door of the school. So this was the new boy. He'd been informed all about him by Mr Christie, his uncle. This was the boy who ran away. The one who told lies. The one who should have started two weeks ago. This was Noel Christie.

Behavioural problems, his uncle had told him. He'd lost his parents in some kind of accident and hadn't been able to come to terms with it yet, he'd said.

Why did he always get children with problems? He had come to this remote school to get away from problems.

The boy, Noel, looked pale as he stepped from the car. A little scared maybe.

This time, the teacher thought, *I won't get involved.*

The teacher, this Mr Darling, had obviously been watching for us from a window, for he was immediately at the door, grinning like an idiot. He looked older than Uncle William – suddenly I was thinking of him as Uncle William! Should that be telling me something . . . ? Or was it just because I didn't know what else to call him? Wouldn't be calling him anything for long. I'd be out of here first chance I got.

The teacher had frizzy iron-grey hair and bright blue eyes. He looked as if he was wearing a steel scouring pad on his head. 'Hello, Mr Christie,' he said, holding out his hand. 'And this must be Noel?'

'I'm not Noel,' I managed to say – but without a lot of conviction. I was beginning to wonder if I was.

Mr Darling lifted an eyebrow that matched his hair exactly, and glanced at Uncle William.

'I'm sorry,' Uncle William said with a shrug of his shoulders. 'I have told you about some of the problems we've had with Noel. At the moment he's insisting I'm not his uncle, and he's not Noel.'

I turned and glared at him. 'You might be somebody's uncle, but you're not mine.' I looked at the teacher. 'He found me on the moors last night. I was being chased by –'

Mr Darling didn't even let me finish. 'The moors are a dangerous place at the best of times. We have the Moorshap Mire up there. It's treacherous. You get trapped in that and you're lost for ever . . . and now there's supposed to be some kind of creature up there too. The pupils aren't allowed to go home without an escort. I can't even let them out at break times. The sooner they catch this creature the better.' He took a deep breath, looked directly at me. 'Did you see it?'

I wanted to tell him I had. Describe it, make my story sound real. But what could I say? A flash of black fur, the slavering of hungry jaws behind me. I shook my head. 'No,' I admitted.

'I didn't see it either,' Uncle William said, in a tone that suggested I was lying. 'I was just frantic when I saw him running.'

He sounded so genuine, I almost believed him. I looked at him again, tried to remember if I had seen him before. Could this man possibly be my uncle?

'I don't blame you,' Mr Darling said. 'One of our pupils has already gone missing. Been missing for over a week now. He's run away before, so we're hoping he'll turn up soon.' He patted my shoulder. 'Well, Noel, why don't you come in and meet the rest of your class mates. All two of them.' He smiled. 'The school is closing down shortly. You'll be sent to the brand-new school a few miles away. Our register of pupils has been dwindling for weeks now. We lost the little ones last week.'

I decided not to argue. What would be the point? Once Uncle William was away, I could seize my chance and run.

The boy and girl in the class were sitting desks apart as if they didn't like each other. The boy was Asian. He flashed me a massive wide grin, all teeth. The girl scowled. It looked as if scowling was her natural expression. Mr Darling put a hand on my shoulder. 'OK, this is Faisal Yusaf and this is Kirsten Stewart. I'd like you to meet the new boy, Noel Christie.'

25

Faisal liked the look of Noel. Since Paul had left – gone missing, run away, got murdered, eaten by the Beast – so many options . . . Anyway, since he had left, Faisal had no one his age in the class. Only Kirsten, and he couldn't stand her. Didn't think of her as human anyway. Noel was his age, and just his size. He hoped he liked football and horror films and – Faisal glanced at Kirsten – he hoped he'd enjoy winding her up as much as Faisal did.

Kirsten didn't like the look of him. He looked dumb – had a vacant air about him, gazing around the class as if he was in a dream. Not interested in anyone else but himself. No help to her at all.

It looked like, once again, she was on her own.

8

I wanted to scream out, 'I am not Noel Christie!'

After he introduced me, Mr Darling even looked at me, hesitated, as if he was waiting for me to do just that. Why didn't I? Because I was so confused, trying to figure out in my head what was happening – who was I?

'Just sit down anywhere, Noel,' the teacher said. But it was Faisal who moved up and beckoned me near him.

'Unfortunately, once you're in here, you're stuck in here, Noel. With this Beast thing going on, it would be too dangerous to venture outside. The police are patrolling the road constantly.' I was sure he said that to reassure Uncle William, for he turned to him then and said, 'Don't worry. He'll be quite safe here. Locked in tight till you come back for him.'

Locked in tight, I was thinking, as if I was a prisoner. Was that why he was willing to leave me here? Because he knew I couldn't run?

'We've all had letters home,' Faisal told me eagerly. 'We can't go anywhere without an escort. We're picked up, we're dropped off. Just like the mail,' he laughed.

'In your case, junk mail,' Kirsten said snootily, and Faisal stuck out his tongue at her.

Everyone dropped off and picked up? What chance of escape from here?

Uncle William stood at the door of the classroom, muttering to the teacher, glancing now and again towards me.

Finally, Uncle William left. I watched him walk round to where the car was parked, in a little parking area out of sight of the door, heard the engine start up and the car drive off. Now was my chance to run . . . but how? I imagined myself pushing my way out of the classroom, fleeing across the moors. The police would be alerted immediately. It would make the papers. The Dark Man would see it. He would find me again. No!

I was brought out of my daydream by the teacher's voice.

'I believe Noel almost encountered the Beast last night, isn't that right, Noel?'

Faisal almost fell off his seat. His eyes went wide, eager to hear all the details. 'Did you? What happened? What did it look like? Did it have horns? Claws? What size was it?'

'One thing's for sure, it can't be half as ugly as you.' It was the girl who said it. She had a snooty little voice. A right little madam. I decided I didn't like her.

Faisal didn't seem in the least offended. Used to her probably. 'Have you looked in the mirror recently, Kirsten? No, I keep forgetting. Every time you look in one you break it, don't you?'

He looked at me and grinned. I had to smile back.

Mr Darling didn't seem too annoyed at them either. He told them to be quiet – that was all.

'Maybe you haven't heard the story of the Beast, Noel.' He looked from Faisal to Kirsten. 'Noel has only just arrived here from . . . Where did you come from, Noel?'

I looked blank, didn't know what to say. Mr Darling answered the question himself. 'London. I think your Uncle William said it was London.'

London? Big place. I waited for something to ring a bell. A memory, but nothing did.

'Yeah,' Faisal said. 'It was London. Your uncle contacted my dad about renting a cottage up here. My dad's an estate agent. In fact he's THE estate agent around these parts. If you want a house, you have to come to my dad.'

'That's only because nobody's daft enough to live here . . . except us.' Kirsten again.

Mr Darling was still going on about the Beast. 'There have always been rumours of some kind of wild creature on the moors, a puma perhaps, but lately things have hotted up. The first new sighting was just a couple of weeks ago. Some climbers claimed they saw something huge lurking up there. Then some sheep were found –'

'Their guts were ripped out. Blood everywhere.' This from Faisal. Kirsten tutted.

Mr Darling shook his head. 'Well, they'd been killed anyway. It's happened again since. So it seems there is something dark and predatory up there on the moors.'

Dark and predatory, only a teacher would describe it like that.

'No one's ever actually seen it. My mum says people are just making it up to frighten someone. It's just one of those urban legends.' This was Kirsten.

'What's an urban legend? 'I asked.

Kirsten looked at me in amazement. 'You don't know what an urban legend is?'

Mr Darling seemed amused. 'Why don't you tell him, Kirsten?'

'An urban legend is one of those stories that goes from one place to another as if it happened there. Like, there's supposed to be a beast roaming in Cornwall. Then you hear about one in Scotland, then one is spotted in the Lake District. Everyone jumping on the bandwagon. There's probably no beast at all.'

'Or did you hear the one about the babysitter, Noel?' Faisal said eagerly.

I shook my head. I had heard nothing.

'This girl was babysitting and she kept getting these phone calls . . . "I'm coming to get you."' Faisal put on an eerie voice. 'Finally, she calls the exchange and they tell her,' – his voice became a yell – '"Get out of that house quick. He's on the phone in the bedroom!" But it's too late. He got her anyway. Cut her into little pieces and ate her.'

I had a feeling Faisal had added that bit on himself.

'That happened in Manchester,' he said.

Kirsten sounded really annoyed. 'It happened in America, Faisal.'

'It's another example of an urban legend,' Mr Darling said to me.

'You know what the latest one is?' Faisal asked. 'The boy with no name who came from nowhere, was responsible for the death of a real villain and saved a town from being blown up and then,' – Faisal snapped his fingers – 'he disappeared into nowhere again. I heard it happened in Edinburgh . . . and then my cousin Abdullah told me it was in Liverpool actually.'

I caught my breath. That boy with no name was me . . . wasn't he?

'That's a made-up story, Faisal Yusaf,' Kirsten said in an annoyed voice. 'You don't believe that could really happen? A boy with no name, who came from nowhere and disappeared into the shadows. Honestly, you watch too many DVDs. Come on. Get real!'

'It's an urban legend.' Faisal turned to the teacher. 'Isn't it, sir?'

'It certainly seems to be heading that way,' Mr Darling said.

'I think it's just a story. A made-up story!' Kirsten was the cynical sort, I thought. Everything would have to be proved before she would believe it. 'Anyway, I don't reckon there's any kind of huge beast out there. My mum should know. She's a scientist. She works at the research facility here.'

Faisal, it seemed, was the total opposite. He was willing to believe everything. 'I don't think it's made up. Some people say it's a puma. I don't think so. A puma wouldn't be big enough. Or fierce enough. I mean, this must be a really big animal. Much bigger than a puma. Killing cows and sheep and deer, as well.' He looked at me, his eyes wide, grinning a flash of even white teeth. 'I think it's a yeti, or Bigfoot. I think somebody's brought it back from abroad and it's escaped.'

Kirsten looked at him in disgust. 'Faisal, you are an

31

idiot. What are you trying to say? You think it's here on its holidays?'

'Might be – two weeks on the moors, all inclusive.'

'Some holiday. People are out trying to shoot the poor thing.'

Mr Darling interrupted her. 'Not to kill it though, Kirsten. They only want to sedate it . . .'

'Study it as if it's a freak! I don't like that either. No wonder the animal-rights preventers are out marching.'

'Ha! Animal-rights protestors, Kirsten.' Faisal turned to me. 'She always gets her words wrong!'

'I think it's cruel. The poor thing laid out on a table, everyone poking at it.'

'Then it suddenly comes to, leaps from the table and eats everybody.' Faisal, of course.

'Serve them all right!' Kirsten said.

'You think it should be allowed to roam free, Kirsten?' Mr Darling asked her.

'It has a right to live as well.'

'Even though it's eating people?' Faisal asked.

Kirsten turned on Faisal. 'Well, if it ate you it would be a bonus for everybody.'

'Anyway, we can be thankful it hasn't attacked any humans yet,' the teacher said.

'Unless it's eaten Paul.' Kirsten said it flatly.

Mr Darling turned to me to explain. 'Paul Wilkie. He was one of our pupils. He went missing almost two weeks ago.'

Just like me, I thought.

Faisal took up the story. 'Paul was always running away. His dad, Wilkie, kept battering him.'

32

'His stepdad,' Kirsten corrected.

'They always caught him, took him back.'

'Well, they haven't caught him this time,' Mr Darling said.

'Hope they don't catch him,' Faisal added. He sounded angry, and I didn't think he often sounded angry. 'I'd have run away from that Wilkie as well.'

'He's better at home surely, than out there on the moors at the mercy of the Beast, Faisal,' Mr Darling said.

And Faisal answered him at once. 'I think Paul would rather take his chances with the Beast.'

Uncle William arrived home.

'Any problems?' Aunt Mary asked him.

'None. He can't leave the school. I don't think he'll even try. The place is swarming with police searching for the Beast. And I told the teacher he has to be watched.'

'We're taking a terrible risk, though.'

'I've warned the teacher Noel tells lies. No one will believe a word he says. I think it's worth the risk, my dear.'

'Is it all going to work out, William?' Aunt Mary looked worried.

He crossed the kitchen and hugged her.

'Of course it is. Don't worry. In a few days it will all be over.'

There was a meeting in another city. The Dark Man was being questioned by his associates.

'There must be a way to find him. We have to find him. What he knows could ruin all our plans.'

'How could you lose him?'

And how could he lose him indeed? He was only a boy. That was what they thought. The Dark Man knew he was something more. He had almost had him, been a hand's breadth away from him, and the boy had leapt from his grasp, disappeared into the shadows. He was resourceful – always had been. He drew on a long cigarette. 'He hasn't gone far. He's on foot. I have my sources. I will find him.'

'You should have killed him when you had the chance,' one of them said.

The Dark Man did not agree with that. 'We have to find out what he knows.'

'You said he has no memory.'

'Nor has he – but for how long? I intend to make sure he can't pass on what he knows.'

He said it with assurance and they were satisfied. For the moment. They were used to him delivering on his promises.

'We don't have much time,' one of the men said.

The Dark Man's eyes narrowed and he said, almost to himself, 'I will get him.'

9

Lunchtime, and we weren't even allowed to leave the building. Mr Darling was watching me like a hawk, ready to leap on me if I made the slightest move to the door, just as he had during morning break.

Regularly, a police car would zoom along the road. The high-profile police presence was for our safety, he assured us. A wild animal was roaming the moors.

What was I more afraid of? The Beast, or Uncle William and Aunt Mary? Those two gave me the creeps. What did they have planned for me?

Faisal sidled up to me, offered me his sandwiches. 'Murder, isn't it?' he said.

I looked at him sharply. 'What?'

'It's murder being cooped up in here. Usually he goes into his house at break times to see his wife. I think he's keeping his eye on you.' He nodded over to Mr Darling, sitting at his desk, looking glum, eating a banana. 'It's like being in prison,' Faisal went on.

'Don't you want to just break the rules? Run outside. I mean, what could they do to you if you did?'

Faisal tapped his chin with his finger as if he was deep in thought. 'Let me see, stay in the building or become the main course for a flesh-eating monster. No contest.' He grinned at me. The boy was an idiot. 'You're the boy who keeps running away, aren't you?'

I wanted to say no. But suddenly, I wasn't so sure who I was.

'You know a lot,' I said instead.

'Heard Mr Darling on the phone to your uncle. You were supposed to start here a couple of weeks ago. You've caused that poor uncle of yours nothing but worry.' He leant closer, whispered, 'You saw it, didn't you?'

'I saw something.' It was out before I could stop myself.

'No one's ever really seen it, you know. You could sell your story to the papers. Wish I could.'

'No, you wouldn't want to see it.' I remembered the fear, the terror. The sound of those jaws snapping close behind me. I was spared more questions from Faisal by Mr Darling calling me over.

'Is everything all right, Noel? You look pale.'

I took a deep breath. 'If I told you I wasn't this Noel, that this time yesterday I'd never even met this Uncle William . . . what would you do?'

'Your uncle told me you'd say all this.'

'What if it's the truth?'

'I could phone the police. They would come here. Investigate.' He stared at me. 'I'll do that if you really want me to.'

I couldn't even hold his gaze. My eyes flicked away from his. I stared out of the window. The fog was coming down again, hemming me in. The police involved. That would mean an investigation. Publicity. The Dark Man on my trail. That was how he'd found me before. Saw the story about me in a newspaper. I had to keep a low profile, till I found out who I really was. I had to stay one step ahead of the Dark Man.

Or was I making all this up, this alternative memory of mine? Maybe I really was this Noel – the boy who keeps running away, who makes up stories. That was the truth of it.

I didn't even have to answer him. My hesitation had been answer enough. I was lying. Mr Darling was sure of it now. 'Thought not,' he said. 'Try to enjoy the classes, Noel. You're practically having one-to-one tuition here. Who knows? You might even enjoy the lessons.'

Kirsten had heard everything. She sat with a smug smile on her face, pretending she was reading her girlie magazine. So, the new boy thought Mr Darling would help him? The teacher was the last person he should have gone to. Even Faisal, thick as a brick, knew that.

The new boy was a liar, and a troublemaker. He kept running away.

But what exactly was Noel Christie running away from?

10

They were studying a war. The whole afternoon, talking about some war I couldn't remember, had never heard of. World War Two. It amazed me, terrified me to think that the whole world could be involved in a war – for a second time. But I said nothing.

And the other horror they were talking about was even worse. A holocaust. A whole race almost wiped out because they were different. Genocide, they called it. Stories that made me feel ill.

And I remembered the book I had read. Anne Frank. And how she and her family had hidden in an attic until they were caught, and she died.

Why did those stories make me so afraid?

'Why were people so evil?' I had tried to keep my mouth shut. Not say a word. Simply listen. But it was out before I could stop myself.

'I'm afraid some were. But, just remember, for every evil person, there are a hundred decent ones, Noel,' Mr Darling said.

I couldn't get used to that name. Noel.

Kirsten didn't seem to agree with him. 'I don't know about that, sir.'

'Oh yes, Kirsten. Look at all the tales of heroism that came out of that war. There was the priest who chose to go into the gas chamber with the children he was looking after, rather than let them die alone. There were people who risked their lives hiding Jews. And what about the people who were in the Resistance in the countries occupied by the Nazis?'

'What was the Resistance?' I was drawn in, in spite of myself.

'Men and women who were willing to risk their lives to see the Nazis defeated. They helped Allied airmen who had been shot down in occupied Europe to escape. They'd hide them, transport them from one safe place to another, from one group to another, until they could get them into neutral territory.'

'I'd have been in the Resistance, sir,' Faisal said.

'Would you, Faisal? You would have to be really brave to be in the Resistance. If you were caught, you would be tortured, perhaps shot for helping the enemies of the Third Reich.'

'I'd still do it,' Faisal said proudly.

'In your dreams, Faisal.' Kirsten laughed. 'One jackboot in the street and you would be running up the swaztikker and shouting, "Heil Hitler!", at the top of your voice.'

Faisal jumped to his feet. 'No, I would not! And it's swastika!'

'I'm not blaming you for that, Faisal. I'd be doing the same, probably five minutes before you!' She laughed again.

'But you're a girl,' Faisal snorted.

'Were the Nazis defeated?' I suddenly couldn't bear the thought that these people were still in charge somewhere.

Kirsten turned on me then, forgot Faisal's insult. 'What planet are you from? Of course they were defeated.'

Mr Darling went on. 'This country was never successfully invaded. So the Allies were able to use this island as their base and thousands of men landed on the beaches in Normandy and took back Europe. A lot of brave men and women died. But the Nazis were defeated.'

Why couldn't I remember any of this? Could he see the relief on my face?

'It was called Operation Overlord, wasn't it, sir?' Faisal said.

'Yes, the plans for the invasion were just about the biggest secret in history. The Germans didn't know where the Allies would land. If they'd found out it was going to be Normandy they would have been waiting for the Allied forces there and the invasion would have failed. You can imagine how hard the Nazis tried to discover that secret.'

The Dark Man after me, my secret. Why was it so important? A voice whispering to me, *You can't let them find out.* The voice so close and clear against my ear that I was sure if I whirled round someone would be there. My past. A memory. But find out what? And who was 'them'? I must have gone pale for Mr Darling asked then, 'Are you feeling OK, Noel?'

'It's . . . a horrible story,' I said.

'My dad says there are still Nazis in the world, sir,' Faisal said.

To my horror, Mr Darling agreed with him. 'That's why we have to treasure our freedom, so people like that can never be so powerful again.'

Nazis. Genocide. Operation Overlord. Was I remembering about this war? For suddenly things were tumbling in my brain – words, memories – so fast I couldn't grasp them . . .

'Expendable.' In a dark room somewhere, I was listening. Hiding behind a curtain, not supposed to be there. 'You can't make an omelette without breaking a few rotten eggs.' And it was the Dark Man who said it. I recognised the coldness in his voice. 'These people are expendable.'

But no one's expendable. Everyone has worth, haven't they?

Suddenly back in that dark room. My leg scraped against a chair. I was afraid, tried to move away, but they heard me. The Dark Man turned, came towards me, pulled the curtain across. He smiled at me. 'Ah, look who's here,' he said.

Black spots in front of my eyes. The room swayed. I shivered with fear.

And then I was back in the classroom. Mr Darling had me by the shoulders. 'You almost fainted there. How are you feeling?'

I tried to answer him, but the words wouldn't come. My mouth too dry. A flicker of a memory gone. But I had been in some faraway room on a day not so long ago, and I had heard something I wasn't supposed to hear. Was that the reason the Dark Man was after me?

'Do you think the new boy is all there?' Kirsten whispered to Faisal as they were preparing to leave.

Faisal looked at her blankly. 'What do you mean?'

'Oh, I know you're not all there, but he's even less all there than you are and that's saying something.'

Faisal thought about that. Realised she'd just insulted him again. 'Because he knows nothing about the Nazis? Come on, he's just not as clever as me.'

'He seems to know nothing about nothing,' Kirsten said. 'And look at the daze he went into. I think there's something weird about him. I'm going to keep my eye on him.'

Uncle William was waiting for me when school was over. All day I had tried to think of ways to run, to get away, but I had been watched the whole time. He was chatting with Faisal's father.

Faisal dragged me over and introduced me to his dad. 'This is my friend, Noel,' he said.

I thought 'friend' was a bit of an exaggeration. Uncle William patted my shoulder, as if he really was my favourite uncle. 'So glad you've made friends already.'

I pulled myself free of him. If Faisal's dad noticed he said nothing. In fact he hardly looked at me at all. Probably thought I was just a bad-tempered schoolboy.

I wished they could see into my mind. See how totally confused I felt. Who was I?

I wished desperately I had someone that I could trust.

Someone I could confide in.

Mr Darling watched them all go. First Kirsten and her mother – that woman was always the last one to turn up. Never got out of the big Jaguar she drove. Didn't even turn off the engine. She pushed the door open for her daughter, hardly ever smiling. No wonder Kirsten was always so miserable herself.

And Faisal and his father. Mr Yusaf was just like Faisal, smiling and talkative. He was talking now to the new boy's uncle.

The new boy. Noel. He drew himself away from his uncle's touch. Why?

No. No more. He was not getting involved. He had given the boy a chance to speak today, and he had turned it down. Because he was lying probably, exactly as his uncle had said he would.

This was not his business.

His mobile rang. His wife, Millie, in the house waiting for him. Once he had been able to confide in her, talk to her about everything. But not now. He wouldn't tell her about Noel. She still hadn't got over Paul.

11

All the way back I stared at the dismal darkening moorland as it sped past. Uncle William kept glancing at me. Why did I keep on thinking of him as Uncle William? Should that be telling me something? Was he really my uncle? He looked concerned. But concerned for what? That I might run away?

As if he was reading my thoughts he said, 'Only danger out there on the moor, Noel.'

I swung round at him. 'Stop calling me Noel. I am not Noel. You don't have to pretend with me.'

His clear blue eyes narrowed. 'I'm not pretending, Noel. Why are you?'

I couldn't answer. I didn't know what to say.

We arrived at the cottage just as the mist was descending on the moor. No full moon tonight. Nothing to be seen tonight.

Aunt Mary was waiting for us. 'I've made you a curry,' she said as soon as I stepped inside. The house was filled with the rich smell of spices.

'Mmm,' Uncle William breathed in the smell. 'Aunt Mary's curry. Just the thing for a night like this.'

Would they be feeding me this well if they meant me

harm? Would they be keeping up this pretence of being my aunt and uncle if it wasn't true?

'Have a good day, Noel?' She glanced at her husband when she said it. I was sure he nodded at her. 'Oh, that's good,' she said, as if I had answered her.

I sat at the table but I had no intention of eating. She put the plate down in front of me and I promised myself I wouldn't touch a thing. It could be drugged – or poisoned. I would not touch it. But I watched her ladle the same curry from the same deep bowl on to her own plate and then on to his. She sat down, began eating. 'Aren't you hungry?' she asked.

He was eating too, grabbing slices of flat bread from a platter and dipping it into the curry sauce.

I couldn't resist it. I got stuck in.

And all the time they talked together just like any other normal people. Nice people.

'The bulb needs changing in the attic, dear. It keeps flickering.'

'I heard a wonderful play on the radio this morning.'

'You must make up some sandwiches for Noel tomorrow, dear. They aren't allowed outside with this Beast business.'

And when they looked at me, they smiled.

And I began to wonder. Was I mad? Or were they?

Later, as I looked out of the window of my room – Noel's room actually – I considered my chances of escape over the moors tonight. Slim to nil. The fog was thick. I would be lost in it in the blink of an eye.

45

And somewhere out there the Beast was roaming wild.

I opened the door of the wardrobe. The clothes inside were all my size. My clothes? I tried hard to remember buying them, wearing them. But nothing came.

Aunt Mary came in with a nightcap. Hot chocolate and toast. I looked around the room. 'Why aren't there any photographs of me?'

She put the tray beside my bed and drew the curtains closed. 'We've only just moved here.' Her eyes went to the ceiling, and beyond to the attic. 'That attic is stacked with boxes we just haven't had time to unpack. Your photos are probably all up there.'

Why did they have to keep coming up with these sensible, logical answers? Because they were telling the truth? That was the thought that kept slapping me in the face. They were telling the truth!

'What happened to my parents?'

She gave out a long dramatic sigh. 'You know they were killed in a car crash. You've found it very hard to deal with that. That's the reason you're having all these problems. But the psychologist says you'll soon be better. We love you, Noel. Uncle William and I will always be here for you.' She smiled again. It was that smile that scared me every time.

'So, if you're my beloved Aunt Mary and Uncle William, and you're so good to me, exactly why do I keep running away?'

In the blink of an eye her smile disappeared. 'Oh, Noel. You're taking this too far. It's not our fault. It's you who can't deal with things, no matter what we try to do

46

to help you.'

She blinked a few times. Was she trying to create tears? I couldn't tell. Then she stormed out of the room, slamming the door behind her.

I stood up and looked in the mirror. I had no past. I didn't know who I was.

But one thing I was sure of, I had to hold on to. No matter what they said . . . I would not believe them.

I was not this Noel!

The mist seemed to cling to the window. Step outside and I would be sucked into it, lost for ever. But I would be lost to Aunt Mary and Uncle William too.

I didn't care. I had to get away. I was going to take my chances on the moor.

12

It surprised me how easy it was to get out of the house. The back door was locked, but the key hung in plain sight on a hook on the wall. I hadn't taken into account how cold it would be. The fog settled around my shoulders like an ice-cold blanket. I took one quick look back at the cottage in darkness. Was I sorry to be leaving it – a warm bed, good food, maybe even a family? Then I pictured Aunt Mary and Uncle William smiling at me and it wasn't the cold that made me shiver. There was something sinister about those two. Even if I really was this Noel, I'd still want to run away from them.

I began to hurry down the misty road. I'd stick to the road, keep away from the moors. If I heard a car heading my way, or anyone coming, only then would I risk stepping off the road. I'd jump behind a thicket of gorse till the danger had passed. But on the road, I'd be safe from this mire they talked about. Safe from the Beast too. The road had to lead somewhere. I was safe on the road.

And suddenly, the road disappeared.

One minute I was pounding along on hard ground, the next I was running over a mound of moss. I retraced my steps carefully. Couldn't see a thing between the dark and the fog. Back, back I went, step by step, sure I must be able to find the hard tarmac of the road again. My foot caught on a broken branch. I stumbled back, trying to keep my balance. No chance. I went down hard. My cheek cracked against stone. I was back on my feet in a second, breathing hard. All I could think of was finding the road again. My face stung. My foot ached. I was only ten minutes on the road and I was lost.

The road had to be here somewhere, steps away from me. But no matter what direction I seemed to go all about me there was only moss and bracken. It was as if I had stepped into another dimension. The road had to be close by. But where? The fog was so thick, the night so black. I could see nothing.

But I could hear.

Somewhere in the distance, a movement. The swish of something in the gorse bushes nearby. I stepped back, but there was only more gorse and moss. I had to get away from that sound. I ran, tripped again, tumbled down an embankment. I clutched at some ferns to stop from falling. Could hear the gush of water below me. A stream. I clung tight, pulled myself up. Lay back on the ground, gasping for breath.

How can a road disappear? I was lost now. I knew it. Disorientated in the darkness. Couldn't find the way back, didn't know the way forward. Was there a safe place I could hide myself till daylight? And even in daylight, would I be able to find the road?

I stumbled on, listening for any sound. The engine of a car, the hoot of an owl. The growl of the Beast.

'He's gone.' Aunt Mary had got up out of her bed to check on him. The way the boy had spoken to her had niggled her awake. She shook her husband. 'I told you we should have had the alarm installed right away.'

'They're doing it tomorrow.' Uncle William stood up. 'Didn't he drink his nightcap?'

'No, it's still lying there along with his toast. He doesn't trust us, remember?' She tugged the curtain at the window open. 'We'll never find him in this fog.' She sounded annoyed.

Uncle William took her by the shoulders. 'I'll get the car and go looking for him.'

'What if the Beast gets him first? You know we can't risk that.'

He said firmly, 'I found him last time. I'll find him again.'

She was just as firm. 'You have to find him, William. It's too soon.'

I found a cleft of rock and snuggled down into it. I drew up my knees and wrapped my arms round them. I was afraid. There was no sound – as if every sound was muffled in the fog. I was in a strange silent world. But there *was* something. I was sure of it. That's why I was afraid. There was something stalking me through the mist. I could sense it coming closer though I couldn't see it.

I tried to brush away the thought. I was being stupid, letting my imagination run away –

I leapt to my feet as an explosion of sound broke the

silence. I was right. Something was out there. What had that sound been? Rocks falling in the distance – a mini avalanche? I turned this way, turned that way. Didn't know which way to run. My foot slipped on moss. I was on the ground again, rolling downhill. I hit hard rock. Had to bite my lip to keep from crying out. I lay still as death, hoping whatever it was would soon pass me by. Miss my scent.

No more sound. Nothing. Had it passed? Was it gone? I don't know how long I lay there. Time seemed to have stopped.

Finally, it seemed a long time later, I risked a step from my hiding place. A movement to ease the pain in my back. Just one step.

And found myself staring down the barrel of a gun.

13

Uncle William drove slowly along the road, fog lights blaring, occasionally sounding his horn. This wasn't supposed to be happening. He tried to stem his panic. He had to find the boy . . . and then what? Drag him back, make him stay? Could they do that? Were they insane even trying it? But he remembered, they had no choice.

The man with the gun looked at the boy. He was dishevelled. Was he the same boy he had seen on the moors a few days before? The same one he'd caught sight of just last night, rescued in the nick of time by a passing car? He wasn't wearing the long coat any more. But he was the same age, had the same colouring. His face glared white now. White with fear.

'What are you doing here? Do you know how dangerous it is here?'

The boy took a deep breath. 'Free country,' he said.

The hunter liked his pluck, snapping back even with a loaded rifle in his face. That took guts.

'There's more than one danger out here,' he said.

'This wild animal . . . and the Moorshap Mire.'

'Heard about them both,' the boy managed to say.

'The Moorshap Mire is treacherous. You'd be lost for ever if you stepped in that.'

He lowered the gun. The boy was no danger. 'Haven't you got a home?' He took a guess. 'Do you live in that cottage on the moors?'

The boy was breathing hard, but he didn't answer. It was as if he didn't know how to answer. 'What's your name?'

And again the boy said nothing, as if he didn't know what his own name was.

'I'll take you to the police,' he decided.

And an answer came at once. 'My name's Noel,' the boy said, his voice quivering.

'And you do live in the cottage?'

The boy nodded. 'I'll go back there now. Just show me the road.'

The hunter smiled. 'I think I can do better than that. I'll take you there.'

'I can find my own way.'

'You think you can find your way in this?'

'I can find my way anywhere,' he said.

But the hunter wasn't taking any chances. He couldn't have a lone boy wandering on the moors tonight.

'You have a choice,' he said. 'Either I take you back home . . . or I take you to the police.'

Why had I told him my name was Noel? I was falling deeper and deeper into this mess, like being dragged down into that blinking Moorshap Mire. It was because he mentioned the police. I couldn't afford to be taken to the police. Couldn't risk that.

I tried to stop myself shaking as I walked behind him. Couldn't. Because, just for a second, I had been sure the man behind the gun was the Dark Man, here to get me.

'I'll always be one step behind you,' he had warned me.

And I was afraid. I could never let the Dark Man get me. I'd go back to Uncle William and Aunt Mary first.

They were almost at the cottage. It lay surrounded by wisps of fog, like something out of a scary tale. A light was on in the downstairs room.

'Looks like someone's up waiting for you, worrying about you.' The hunter looked at the boy. 'Go on.'

The boy looked at him. 'Aren't you coming in with me?'

'Don't worry, I won't leave till you're safely inside.'

'Making sure I don't run again?' he asked. He looked at the rifle. 'Are you after the Beast?'

'Isn't everybody?' the hunter answered.

The boy watched him. 'But not with real bullets.'

He took a moment to answer him. 'Now, how would you know that?'

This time the boy said nothing. It was as if his face was set in stone. He held his gaze, didn't look away, until he turned and walked down the path to the warm light of the cottage, walking towards that light as if it was the hardest thing he ever had to do.

Yet he'd given the boy the chance to leave. Suggested they go to the police together. What was he hiding?

He waited till the boy was inside the cottage before he turned and strode back into the fog. He had other things to concentrate on. He had got it at last. He was sure of it this time. Now, all he had to do was find it.

Uncle William rushed back into the house. He was panicking by now. 'Couldn't find him anywhere.' Then he noticed that Aunt Mary was smiling. 'Is he back?' he asked her.

Her smile was all teeth. 'An hour ago. Wouldn't talk. Went straight to bed.'

'What made him come back?'

Aunt Mary shrugged. 'Don't know. Don't care. He's back. It's going to work out, William. This time it is all going to work out.'

I lay in bed, glad of the warmth, glad of the comfort, wishing I was anywhere else but here. What had made me come back? Why did they want me? And who was the mysterious man with the rifle? A rifle with real bullets. He had asked me how I knew that. How *had* I known that?

I sat up in bed. I realised all at once that it was a shot I had heard through the fog. Not rocks falling at all, but a shot.

And how could I be so sure . . . unless I had heard shots before? Where? I even felt a gun in my hand, my fingers wrapped around a trigger. Something darted into my mind, so close I felt I could reach out and touch it. Then it was gone. My memory? Or my warped imagination?

The man with the gun . . . had he killed the Beast?

I lay back down and was drifting into uneasy sleep when I heard it.

The howl of a wild animal, but this was no ordinary wild animal. This was a howl of the Beast. A sound that tore at me. It sounded angry, and heartbroken.

The Beast still alive.

So if he hadn't killed the Beast . . . what had he killed?

14

TUESDAY

The boy, Noel Christie, was back. He sat in the class-room beside Faisal. His eyes had a hunted look in them. His face was bruised as if he'd fallen. Mr Darling wanted to reach out and touch his shoulder, ask him to confide in him. Maybe the boy *had* tried to confide in him yesterday, and he had turned away. But he couldn't get involved any more. He'd got into enough trouble the last time. It had cost him no end of problems, trying to help Paul. He had promised himself, he had promised Millie, that it would never happen again.

'Did you hear it last night?' Faisal nudged the boy, Noel, to get his attention. It took quite a few nudges to get him to turn round. He was away in another world, staring out of the window. 'That howl during the night? Did you hear it? You couldn't have missed it. It woke me up.'

Noel's eyes were glassy. Maybe for once, Faisal thought, Kirsten had hit the nail on the head: the new boy wasn't all there. There was definitely something funny about him anyway.

57

'Woke me up too,' he said at last, as if it was an effort. 'What happened to your face?'

The boy ran his fingers over the purple bruise on his cheek. 'I tripped and fell.'

Faisal wasn't sure if he believed that. 'Are you feeling OK?' Faisal was beginning to think perhaps Noel was sick. Maybe the so-called fall had left him with concussion. He was ready to call out to Mr Darling – who knows, he might need an ambulance? Faisal imagined the boy collapsing on the floor, the siren wailing through the glen, white-coated paramedics rushing in, giving him oxygen, putting him on a drip – a little bit of much-needed drama.

But after a moment the boy just shrugged his shoulders. 'I'll be fine,' he said.

But he wasn't fine, Faisal could see that. He had dark circles under his dark eyes. Eyes that seemed a million miles away.

Faisal sat back with a sigh. Why couldn't he get a decent mate? He was a friendly boy. He'd been as friendly as he could with Paul, tried to help him. But Paul had had so many problems, always running away, getting caught, being brought back. As if he was attached to the place with elastic.

But he hadn't come back this time, Faisal reminded himself. Was he safe somewhere far away . . . ? Or, and this seemed more likely, was he somewhere out on the moors, stiff as a board. Maybe he was lying deep in the Moorshap Mire, or even worse, was he a victim of the Beast?

Faisal glanced across at Kirsten. She was sitting there,

her nose stuck in the air. She believed, because her mother was a scientist, she was better than him, better than anybody. He could never get on with her.

Faisal had thought yesterday that he might have a pal in the new boy. Today, he wasn't so sure. He had a funny feeling Noel Christie wouldn't be here much longer either.

'Noel! You're not paying attention! Noel!'

It took a moment for me to realise that the teacher was talking to me. Noel. I wanted to yell at him, 'I am not Noel. My name is . . .'

But what was my name?

Ram? I'd made that up, hadn't I? Or had I? Or was I really this Noel?

I had woken up more confused than ever this morning. What had made me come back to the cottage last night? I had let myself be led back there as if it was home. I had even said my name was Noel. Was that really because I was trying to protect myself from this mysterious Dark Man? Or was he just someone I had made up in this crazy mind of mine? I was beginning to think I didn't know what was real and what wasn't.

At breakfast Uncle William and Aunt Mary hadn't said a word about my disappearance during the night. Neither had I. They couldn't have been nicer, chatting over breakfast – bacon, eggs, sausages, extra helpings of anything I wanted – talking about ordinary everyday things. He had to get the car washed, she wondered if her shopping could be delivered, and I began to think, to wonder that maybe I was going mad. Maybe I needed some kind of special treatment. There was something wrong inside my head.

'Noel!'

I looked up at Mr Darling. He looked concerned. 'Noel, are you feeling OK?'

'That's what I asked him, sir,' Faisal said eagerly. 'I think he looks sick.'

The girl tutted. 'Oh, listen to our medical expert. He knows everything, of course.'

'I know more than you, smartie pants,' Faisal threw back.

'Well, Noel? How are you feeling?'

I thought about it. If I said I didn't feel well, I'd be sent home. A day with Uncle William and Aunt Mary? Couldn't handle that. I had more chance of escape here.

I sat up straight. 'I'm fine, sir.'

'Don't suppose you heard a thing we were discussing?'

The teacher was right. I hadn't been listening. Faisal filled me in.

'Conspiracies – we were talking about conspiracies.'

Conspiracies? I wasn't even sure what that meant.

'There was a conspiracy to assassinate Hitler during the war,' the teacher explained.

'Did it work?' I was sorry I asked the second it came out.

Kirsten turned on me. 'Duh! Did it work? Are you for real?' She sucked in her cheeks and rolled her eyes. I almost asked, was she for real?

Faisal nudged me. 'Thinks she knows everything.'

Mr Darling said to Kirsten. 'Go on, Kirsten. Tell us

what happened.'

'Some of Hitler's generals wanted to stop the war, get rid of Hitler. So they got together, decided to blow him up, but the bomb went off too soon or something, and they were all caught. Murdered horribly. Conspiracies never work.' She finished as if she was angry about that.

'There have been conspiracies all through the ages. The plot to kill Caesar was one of them.'

'Sometimes, people don't even believe there is a conspiracy.' Faisal wanted to sound as clever as Kirsten. I found myself almost smiling.

'And what do you mean by that, Faisal?' Mr Darling sat on the edge of the desk to listen. He looked as if he enjoyed these class discussions. He was a nice man. The thought came to me again – should I try to confide in him one more time?

Faisal went on eagerly. 'Look at John F. Kennedy. They say only one man was to blame for his assassination.'

'Lee Harvey Oswald,' Kirsten said smugly.

Faisal ignored her. 'Everybody knows there was a conspiracy. One man manages to shoot the President of the United States? I don't think so.'

'But who could have been behind such a conspiracy?' the teacher asked.

'Well, I don't really know.' Faisal went on as if he was an expert, 'Everybody had a motive. The Mafia, the Russians, even the people that didn't like him in America.'

'Or maybe they all got together just to get rid of JFK,' Kirsten said as if it was nonsense.

Mr Darling looked at me, waiting for me to join in. I stared back at him blankly. I had never heard of John F. Kennedy. And yet, something was stirring in my brain.

Conspiracy . . . *The Dark Man showing me into a room. Who were those people? Their faces were blurred as they sat in solemn silence, watching me. But I could sense their disapproval, even their anger. I was afraid, but with the Dark Man at my side I realised something else. Something I couldn't understand.*

I felt safe. Protected. The Dark Man would protect me . . .

Safe, with the Dark Man? What was all that about?

I was so mixed up I wanted to scream. Was I making all this up? Having some kind of recurring nightmare?

Who am I?

Mr Darling touched my shoulder. 'You've gone pale, Noel. I could call a doctor if you don't feel well.'

I shook my head. *Pull yourself together, whoever you are,* I told myself.

Faisal was staring at me as if he hoped I would suddenly faint at his feet. He looked disappointed when I didn't.

'You were going to say something, Faisal,' Mr Darling turned from me.

'There are still conspiracies, sir,' Faisal went on, wanting to prove his point. 'That bombing in London. They said it was one man – he blew himself up in the process.'

'And a good thing too!' Kirsten said. 'At least he didn't kill the Prime Minister, or the Cabinet. He wanted to bring down the whole government, the country. That was his plan.'

'Well, my dad says he thinks that was a conspiracy. There were lots of people involved, but only one man gets the blame.'

'The lone gunman,' Mr Darling said thoughtfully. 'That's what they call the theory.'

'You'll be telling us next that men didn't really land on the moon. That it was all filmed in Arizona!' Kirsten said.

This time I couldn't keep quiet. 'Men landed on the moon!'

They all looked at me as if I was crazy. I tried to smile. 'I still can't believe it. Men really did land on the moon.'

And the thought of it seemed to make up for all the horrors I had been learning about.

'And of course, there's the one about Elvis too,' Kirsten said.

Faisal laughed. 'He's not dead. My cousin, Abdullah, saw him in Lockerbie last week.'

The teacher turned to me, waiting for me to add something to this discussion. 'What do you think, Noel?'

'Elvis . . . was he the Prime Minister?'

Kirsten exploded with laughter. 'He doesn't know who Elvis is? Are you sure you don't come from another planet?'

I was trying to think of an answer. It amazed me too – and scared me – the things I could remember and the things I'd forgotten. But I didn't have to think about it for long. There was the wail of a siren coming closer. We all tensed, listening, waiting for the police car to roar past the school. But it didn't. We heard it turn on to the school drive and come to a halt right outside the door.

Mr Darling was out of the room fast. 'I want you to discuss other conspiracies now.'

Nobody did. We leapt from our seats, flew to the window. Mr Darling was outside speaking to an officer. His face was ashen. They only spoke for a moment. Then the policeman was back in the car and the car drove back on to the road.

'Bet they've caught the Beast,' Faisal said, his voice full of excitement.

'Or shot the poor thing,' Kirsten said, as if she didn't approve.

And I remembered the man with the gun, and the shot I had heard. And the wail of a creature in the night. He had shot something, but I didn't think it was the Beast.

We could hardly wait for the teacher to come back into the class. 'What did they want, sir?'

'Have they caught the Beast?'

It took Mr Darling an age to answer. So long, that Faisal and I exchanged glances, wondering what he was about to say.

Finally, he looked directly at us and I could see the light catching the tips of tears in the teacher's eyes. 'They've found a body on the moors. The body of a boy. They think it might be Paul.'

15

Mr Darling wanted to send them home. They should be home, safe with their own families. But he had been told by the police to keep them in the schoolhouse. It was really him who wanted to be home. Home with his wife. He wondered how she would take this news. Not well.

He had watched his pupils' faces when he broke the news. Typically, Faisal's eyes had almost popped out of their sockets. Excited, appalled, scared. It was all an adventure to him. Boys going missing, wild animals on the loose, roaming the moors, and now, a body.

Surely not Paul's? That couldn't be the end for that poor, pathetic young boy? The teacher was trying to hold himself together, finding it hard. He should have helped Paul. He should have done more, was all he kept thinking.

Was that what Kirsten was thinking too? Her cheeks had flushed when she heard the news. He had seen shock on her face. Or was it shame? She hadn't been very nice to Paul, pulling her skirt away from him when he sat close to her, as if she might catch something from him. Was she remembering that too?

But it was the new boy, Noel – it was his reaction that

puzzled him most. He had hardly looked up. As if the news was no shock to him. As if dead bodies were nothing new in his life.

'Is it definitely Paul, sir?' Faisal asked.

Kirsten swung round at him. 'Well, of course it must be Paul. Paul goes missing. Body found on moors. Must be him. Right, sir?'

How could he tell them? The body had been savaged so badly, half eaten, identification impossible at the moment. The police had told him all this, but how could he tell sensitive children anything so horrible?

'If the Beast got him, they wouldn't be able to identify him, would they?' It was the new boy who said it – calmly, as if the thought neither excited nor bothered him.

Faisal nodded. 'Wow! You're right!' The excitement suddenly died from his eyes. 'Hope it wasn't Paul, sir. He didn't deserve that.'

Mr Darling hoped, prayed it wasn't Paul either. Hoped Paul was far away from here, somewhere safe.

But that was a forlorn hope. It had to be Paul. What other boy had gone missing?

I couldn't take my eyes from the teacher. His face was drained of colour. He looked like a waxwork dummy. One of his pupils had been found dead on the moors. It could have been me last night. Except I was saved by the man with a gun. What had he been doing on the moors last night? Hunting for the Beast, yes. But there were already people out searching for it. There would be more now, panning out across the moors.

Mr Darling's mobile rang. He answered it immediately, made an apology and asked us to study our history before he hurried out of the room.

Faisal swung round to me at once. 'It had to happen sooner or later. The Beast kills a human. Now it has a taste for human flesh.'

'Do you really think it's this Paul?'

Faisal's face crumpled. 'I don't want it to be Paul. If anybody was going to kill him, I thought it would be his stepdad. But I suppose he could have left him out on the moors, left him for the Beast, so it could . . .'

Faisal couldn't go on. The thought of it, what had happened to Paul, sickened him. He wanted justice. He wanted revenge.

'It has to be Paul!' Kirsten snapped out. 'Who else could it be?'

Faisal turned on her. He was angry, and that didn't seem to be like Faisal at all. 'You wouldn't care, would you? You were never nice to him.' He turned back to me then. 'She was horrible. Made him feel this high.' He held his finger and thumb an inch apart.

'You didn't do anything to help him either!' she snapped back.

'At least I tried to be his pal,' Faisal said. 'Nobody cared about him, what was happening to him. He kept getting sent back, couldn't take it any more.'

Mr Darling came back into the class then. He looked at me. 'Your uncle's just rung, Noel. He'd heard about the body being found, was worried about you. Wanted to know if he could come and pick you up. I told him the

67

police have advised you all stay here until your usual home time.'

I nodded.

'It's good to know you have someone who cares about you, Noel.' His eyes moved from me to Faisal and then Kirsten. 'You all have people who care about you. Paul never did.'

I had people who cared about me. Was that really what I had? Maybe I really was this Noel? Why should I doubt it? Fight against it? I had no memory of being anyone else. Everything they said fitted in. I lied. I made up stories. So many, that now I couldn't tell what was real and what wasn't. I'd run away. Now I was back. They'd done nothing to harm me, this Uncle William and Aunt Mary. They treated me well. Fed me even better. Why was I questioning their motives? And if their smiles gave me the creeps, maybe the fault was in me, not them.

I had wanted a home, family. Now I had both. Safe in a warm comfortable house. Safe from the Beast on the moors.

I was going to go with the flow.

I was going to be Noel Christie.

16

Mary heard it on the radio. 'They've found a body.' Her voice trembled.

'I know. I heard it too. Don't worry,' her husband said.

'Are you sure, William?'

William smiled. 'Of course. I've already called the school. We have our Noel, and he's safe.'

All day sirens wailed by the school. Every time a police car roared past I froze, expecting that any minute they would screech to a halt, that they were coming for me.

'Don't look so scared,' Faisal told me. It was lunchtime and we sat together in the schoolhouse, eating our sandwiches. A perfect time for me to escape. Today Mr Darling had decided to have his lunch in the house with his wife as usual. He wasn't watching me. But how could I go with so much police activity around?

And anyway, why would I want to? I was Noel Christie. I repeated it to myself over and over again, determined to believe it. I *was* Noel Christie. There was no Dark Man. All that had been a nightmare, a made-up

69

story, best forgotten.

The sandwiches Aunt Mary had made up for me were thick with chicken, and I had hot soup too, in a flask tucked into my rucksack.

She must be my aunt, I was thinking. Why else was she being so good to me? I was going to try to get used to being this Noel. I would have to.

Faisal nudged me. 'Are you listening? What's wrong with you? You jump every time a car comes by.'

Kirsten, sitting in front of us, had been listening. 'Have you got something to hide?'

'Of course I haven't.' I said it quickly. Too quickly. I sounded guilty.

Suddenly, she asked something I wasn't expecting. 'Are they bad to you?'

I stared at her. Wondered why she was asking such a thing. 'No,' I said, and it was the truth. Maybe if she'd asked that yesterday, or even this morning, I would have told her all. Told her that I'd been picked up on the moor, that I wasn't Noel Christie, that I didn't know who I was.

But now? Now I realised I must be this Noel. My memory was blank, but I was Noel Christie. I had to be.

'She's asking that because you keep running away . . . just like Paul,' Faisal said.

'We didn't have to ask if they were bad to him,' Kirsten said. 'He came in every day with bruises. We knew. They all knew.'

'I've not got any bruises.' I pushed the arm of my sweater up to let them see for themselves. I touched my face. 'Except for this one. I fell. I really did fall.' I wanted them to believe that. 'Why did they keep sending Paul back?'

Kirsten smirked. 'Couldn't possibly break up a family, could they?' She put on a simpering voice. '"We'll send social workers in, and family counsellors. Paul will never be afraid again."' Then she pretended to spit on the ground. 'Rubbish! Whenever the social workers came his mother and her new husband would say he was out, or he was sound asleep and they didn't want to disturb him, and then they would move somewhere new and all those social workers couldn't find them . . . till the next time.'

'Paul fell through a crack in the system,' Faisal said. 'That's what my dad says.'

'Someone should have helped him,' I said. I was angry too. I'd never met this Paul, never would, but someone should have helped him.

'Mr Darling tried,' Faisal said. 'He offered to take Paul in.'

'Mrs Darling wanted to look after him,' Kirsten said. 'To contemplate for their dead son.'

'Compensate,' Faisal corrected her, and she glared at him.

'Anyway, that only caused trouble,' she went on. 'Paul's stepdad, Wilkie, came rushing here and had a terrible fight with Mr Darling.'

'What happened to the Darlings' son?' I asked.

'He died. He would be our age now. Some terrible disease,' Kirsten said. 'I don't think Mrs Darling's ever got over it.'

Problems and mysteries, I thought. Everyone seemed

to have them, even here on the moors, remote from everything.

Kirsten was still staring at me. 'I still think there's something suspicious about you.'

Faisal whispered when she'd turned round again, 'Whatever you do, don't trust her.'

I would have nothing to trust her with, I decided. I had no secrets. I was Noel Christie.

Uncle William was waiting outside the schoolhouse. He came out of the car and walked over to where Faisal's father was standing. The girl's mother was there too, sitting in her car, aloof and unsmiling like her daughter.

'Do they know who the body belongs to?' she asked no one in particular. She didn't step from the car, only slid down the window. Kept the engine running. She answered the question herself. 'Must be that boy who's missing. Must be him.'

Uncle William agreed immediately. 'I can't think who else it might be.'

'Not necessarily.' Faisal's father was a small rotund man. He wore thick glasses and nodded his head a lot. 'We have so many hikers on the moors, and there are other boys on the run. Let's not jump to conclusions.'

'They say it will take days to identify him,' the woman said, and she shivered. It had to be from the late-afternoon air, Uncle William decided, because this Mrs Stewart didn't look the type to let a decomposing, half-eaten corpse bother her.

'Maybe the school should close,' Uncle William said.

'They should all be kept at home.'

Faisal's dad waved his hands about. 'No, no. Better they come to school. We know where they are, they are well looked after, and their education is very important.'

Faisal's father looked the type who would say that.

'We take them here,' he went on. 'We collect them. We know they are safe. Anyway, we have no real proof there is such a thing as "the Beast". No one has actually seen it. It's silly to overdramatise. The boy may have died of exposure up there on the moors this time of year. And there are other wild animals that might have . . .' He couldn't go on. Didn't have to. They all knew what he meant.

Kirsten's mother didn't want Kirsten off school either – for her own reasons, Uncle William was sure. 'I couldn't take time off to stay at home with Kirsten. I'm very busy at the moment, and my husband's away on business. He won't be back until next week.'

So the boy must come to school. For the rest of the week at least. He wouldn't keep him at home if the others came. Uncle William would do nothing to arouse suspicion.

The door of the schoolhouse opened and they all came hurrying out. The boy, Faisal, animated and excited, rushed to his dad and began babbling about the body on the moors. The girl, Kirsten, her blonde hair bouncing on her shoulders, walked behind him, a diminutive version of her mother, wearing the same bored expression. She didn't say a word to her mother, just climbed into the passenger seat of the car and sat there, staring ahead.

And last out, taking him by surprise, the boy. He came towards Uncle William, not walking but running, his face all smiles. 'Hi, Uncle William.'

'Look who I've brought home,' Uncle William said as soon as we stepped into the kitchen.

'Hello, Aunt Mary.'

She dropped her spoon into the bowl of stew she was making. I could smell it, and it was delicious. She blinked and came towards me. Her eyes darted to Uncle William, then back to me. She clutched at her chest dramatically. 'Oh, it does my heart good to hear you call me that.'

I backed away, didn't want her to hug me, and there looked a good chance she would do just that. 'I'm sorry for all the trouble I've caused you. I can't seem to remember things too well.'

She beamed at me. 'You will. It will all come back. Now, this calls for a celebration. Chocolate ice cream . . . with walnuts! What do you say to that?'

'Sounds good to me, Aunt Mary.'

So I Uncle-Williamed and Aunt-Maryed them all night. Felt good. I had a family. Why had I fought against it?

As we ate dinner, second helpings were ladled on to my plate. The radio blared out the news about the body they'd found.

'It'll be on television too,' Uncle William said. 'But we don't have TV. Reception's bad. You don't miss it, do you, Noel?'

How can you miss what you don't remember? I shook my head. 'Doesn't bother me,' I said.

Aunt Mary leapt to her feet. Dessert was ready. 'Let's switch it off. I can't bear to hear any more.' She clutched at my hand. 'You won't try to run away again, Noel? That could have been your body they found out there.'

But my nights of running away were over. I was home.

Someone else was listening to the news. In a town, not so far away. The Dark Man.

A body found on the moors. Right age. A boy. Unidentified.

It had only been days since he'd left the riverside town. He could have made it to that moorland, heading south. Sleeping rough in the open. Perfect prey for this Beast they claimed was roaming wild.

His associates wanted to believe the body was the boy's. That he was dead. Gone. A problem solved. They would never find out what he knew, but neither would anyone else.

He would head for this town. It wasn't far. He could be there by morning.

17

I went to bed early. Lay deep in soft sheets and pulled my duvet tight around me and surveyed my room.

My room. I savoured the luxury of having something that was mine. I looked at the posters on the walls – motorbikes, fast cars – tried to remember loving them. But nothing came.

I studied them for ages, trying to remember, desperately wanting something to spark in my memory. But still nothing came.

I had wanted to ask them so much as we ate dinner. Fill me in with my past. Why had we moved here? What kind of people had my parents been? But I couldn't bring myself to tell them I still had no memory of any of them at all.

If only there were photographs. That was strange. No photo of my mother or father. Not even one of Uncle William and Aunt Mary.

She brought me in hot chocolate laced with cinnamon, fluffed up my pillows, tucked me in. Why had I ever doubted her?

'It would be nice to have a photo in here . . .' I didn't want to add that I wanted a photograph of my parents.

'We'll get all that sorted at the weekend. Now you get some sleep.' She bent and kissed my brow. I could smell her perfume, lavender and lilac. Made me feel queasy.

'I'm shattered,' I said, not lying – sure as soon as my head hit the pillow I would be sound asleep.

'Don't forget to drink up your nightcap,' she whispered as she closed the door.

I didn't want to hurt her feelings, but hot chocolate made me feel queasy too. I looked around for somewhere to dump it. There was a pot plant on the corner unit by the door. I wouldn't need her nightcap to help me sleep anyway, I thought as I poured the hot chocolate out. I didn't need anything that night to make me sleep.

Didn't happen that way. I closed my eyes and my head was suddenly filled with everything that had happened since I came here. Something black and sleek and hungry behind me, getting closer every second. A missing boy. A dead body. I tossed and turned, even tried counting sheep, but the sheep kept turning into wild, alien creatures, and there was a man with a gun aimed at them, shouting, 'It's a conspiracy. I'm not the lone gunman.'

Eventually, I gave up. My mind too full for sleep. I sat up in bed, watched the moonlight drift into my room as the clouds parted.

I could hear them still downstairs, playing music, they sounded happy. Did I have anything to do with that, I wondered? At last they had their beloved nephew, Noel, back.

She had said the photographs would be in the attic. I

was sure if I saw those photographs the floodgates of my memory would open and everything would come rushing back to me. All my memories of being Noel Christie would return. It would only take a minute for me to climb up there and explore. They never had to know. Probably wouldn't mind anyway. We were going to sort the photos out at the weekend. I'd be helping them, wouldn't I? Anyway, they'd understand I was curious. But being secretive seemed to come naturally to me.

I slipped out of bed silently.

I was going to find the photographs.

Downstairs Aunt Mary and Uncle William really were celebrating. 'More champagne, dear?' He was already filling her glass.

'This is all going so much better than we'd hoped.'

'Better than last time,' Uncle William said.

'Don't talk about that. We had such bad luck, dear.'

Uncle William filled his glass and sat down beside her. 'Everything's all right now.'

Aunt Mary giggled, sipped more champagne. 'All right now.' She snuggled up to her husband. 'We are clever.'

A stair creaked as I stepped on it. I stopped, held my breath, expecting one of them to hear, hurry up the stairs.

But no one came. I could still hear their murmured voices below, giggling, laughing, happy.

Anyway, what was I worried about? This was my house. I wasn't doing anything wrong. Why was I so jumpy? Old habits die hard.

The attic was musty, piled high with boxes. How would I find anything in here? I fumbled for the light switch, found it hanging from a cord dangling from the bulb. I pulled it on and the room was dimly lit by the solitary bulb, swinging back and forth, back and forth, sending eerie shadows into the corners.

The boxes were all marked in black felt tip.

CHINA: FRAGILE

KITCHEN UTENSILS

BED LINEN

I had to bend down to read each one. The skylight window in the attic looked out over the blackness of the moor. The fog had lifted and I could see the moon, on the wane now, hanging low over the hills. There was more light from that moon than from the pitiful bulb inside. I got down on my knees and began moving boxes aside.

POTS AND PANS

GLASSES

RUGS

This house must have come fully furnished, since none of the things you would imagine they would need every day had been unpacked. And I wondered again – why had we moved here, to somewhere so remote?

Maybe tomorrow I could ask. Find out in such a way it wouldn't sound suspicious at all.

'Don't you get lonely here, Aunt Mary?' I would ask innocently.

And she would reply, 'Now and again.'

'I'll never really understand why we came here,'

And I would lead her into telling me everything.

I was so busy imagining the scene I almost missed the box.

PHOTOGRAPHS

The box was sealed, but it was nothing to rip the tape off. I lifted the lid. Inside, there were more boxes. Chocolate boxes, shoe boxes, tin boxes, cardboard boxes, biscuit tins, all filled with photographs.

And then, right at the bottom I found the box I was sure would help me. A tartan shortbread tin with FAMILY SNAPS printed on a label on the top.

Family snaps.

Surely I had to be in some of them. I lifted out the box and began flicking through the photographs. Some were so old they were tinted yellow. Old Victorians stared back at me glumly, all dressed in their Sunday best. There was a posed photo of a soldier in uniform, standing proudly. Then there were more modern photos: children playing at a beach, a teenage girl in a mini skirt, with a gap in her teeth. And then one of a group of people standing together, dressed up, like for a wedding or something. I peered closer, wished the light was stronger. Was that Uncle William? Had to be. Who could mistake that smile? And there, beside him was Aunt Mary.

And the boy in front of them . . . looking miserable . . . was that . . . ?

Suddenly, the bulb flickered. The light went out.

18

Kirsten watched her mother pull her coat on. 'You're not going out tonight, are you?'

'I have to, Kirsten,' her mother said. 'You'll be fine here. I know I can trust you to stay indoors.'

'Why have you got to go out?! Where are you going?'

Her mother didn't answer that. Why was she always being so mysterious lately? 'I'll only be gone for an hour,' she said.

'I'm too young to be left on my own,' Kirsten made one last attempt to keep her in the house. 'I'm sure it's against the law.'

Her mother came and kissed her head. 'Oh Kirsten. You know you're perfectly capable of looking after yourself.'

Kirsten heard a car coming down the drive. Her mother stepped to the door. 'An hour max,' she said. And then she was gone.

She wished she knew what her mother was up to, the meaning behind all the furtive phone calls she'd been making after Kirsten had gone to bed.

She had another man, Kirsten was sure of it. That was why her dad had left. She glanced out of the window.

Her mother was climbing into a car and although Kirsten couldn't see the driver, she knew it was a man. Her new boyfriend. Had to be.

She went back and sat in front of the television, trying to watch it.

Well, she hadn't taken the Jaguar, Kirsten thought. That was at least one consolation.

Aunt Mary saw the moon from the window. 'Fog's lifted. The moon's bright. He might try to run again.'

'You saw him tonight,' Uncle William squeezed her hand reassuringly. 'He's happy.'

'Maybe,' she said. 'Or maybe he's just a good actor.'

'He's not acting. He's convinced now.'

Aunt Mary turned to him with a smile. 'He won't get the chance to run away anyway. I had the house alarmed today.'

I had taken the photograph back to my room. Had no choice, couldn't see it clearly enough up in the attic, even by the light of that moon. Uncle William obviously hadn't fixed that flickering bulb Aunt Mary had told him about. I had made it back to my room in the nick of time, slipped into bed and put the photo under my pillow just as Aunt Mary knocked on my door and came in.

'I saw your light on, dear. Can't you sleep?'

Her eyes flicked round the room. Why couldn't I just tell her I'd taken a photograph from the box in the attic? Why didn't I just show her the photo?

I lifted a book from the bedside table as if I was reading it. 'Can't put this down,' I said.

'Hansel and Gretel? I didn't think it would be your kind of thing.'

'I love reading,' I lied, forgetting that I didn't know what I loved.

'I know it won't even occur to you, dear,' Aunt Mary sat on the bed, patted my hand, 'but just to let you know I had the house alarmed today. Up here on the moors, so remote, and with this creature on the loose, you can't be too careful.'

So the house was alarmed. No escape. Didn't matter now. 'Good idea,' I said.

Now was my chance to ask her why we've moved here. But I was too eager to get back to that photograph.

She patted down my hair. 'It's so nice having you back, dear.'

I waited till their movements and murmurs had silenced next door. Till I was sure they were in bed, asleep. I waited till all was quiet before I drew the photograph out from under my pillow.

I took the bedside lamp, with its car headlights, under the covers with me. Switched it on.

The family photo had the names of the members written in pen on the back.

Nan. Nan's friend, Jessie. Uncle William, Aunt Mary, Noel . . .

So, it was me. At last, a picture from my past, giving me a family. Surely this would spark a memory. I'd take one look at this photograph and it would be like a dam bursting in my mind. I would remember everything.

My hand was shaking as I turned the photo over slowly.

I let my eyes drift to the dark-haired boy in the front row. I stared at him for a long time.

Noel Christie.

I didn't know who this boy was, but he certainly wasn't me.

19

How was I supposed to sleep after that?

I wasn't Noel Christie.

Just as I was slipping into a new identity, believing I had found a family who cared, I realised instead I had nothing. Again.

I was living his life but I wasn't Noel Christie! I rocked back and forth on the bed, wanted to cry. My throat ached holding the tears back. But I wouldn't cry. What good did crying ever do?

I had been a fool to believe it anyway.

I thought about Uncle William and Aunt Mary, and those creepy smiles, and I wondered why they wanted me. Why were they pretending I was this Noel? What were they up to? I couldn't understand it. They had done me no harm. In fact, they had fed me, kept me warm and safe. I'd even seen how happy they were that at last I believed I was Noel. No, maybe it hadn't been happiness I had seen in those sinister smiles. It had been relief. But why? Who was this Noel?

I knew now I had to get away somehow. But not tonight. I wouldn't have a chance with the new alarm system installed. Couldn't even run from the car, with the child lock. Trapped in a school hemmed in by a police cordon, and a deadly mire. And just to make things worse, the icing on the cake, a wild beast on the moors with a taste for human flesh.

Wow! What else could go wrong for me?

Yet I had to get away. Somehow, I was sure my life depended on that.

The Dark Man switched on the fog lights of his car. He couldn't see a thing ahead of him. He should have waited till morning, perhaps. The fog would have lifted by then. But he had no time to waste. He peered through the gloom. Morning was coming. He would stop at the first house he came to, find out where there was a hotel, find out what people knew about the body on the moors.

'You look pale, Noel. Didn't you sleep well?' Aunt Mary was already putting a plate piled high with bacon and egg and sausage in front of me. I couldn't let them see I knew I wasn't this Noel. I had to keep up the pretence that I believed them. Or I'd never escape.

I smiled back at her. 'Bad dreams.' I said it and it wasn't a lie. My life was filled with bad dreams.

'You poor thing. Eat up. You'll feel better.' Aunt Mary's answer to everything: food.

I looked at the plate on the table. I had to give her credit – Aunt Mary made a great fry-up. Oh well. At least they were feeding me well. I began to tuck in.

'Uncle William's just getting the car out of the garage, heating it up for you.'

Heating the car for me! What was this all about? And the thought struck me again: were these two mad?

She was suddenly alert at a sound in the driveway. Another car. 'Who can that be?'

I heard the car crunch to a halt on the gravel outside. The police, I thought at first, with more news of the dead boy. Aunt Mary – well, what else could I call her? – looked out of the window. Her face crumpled with curiosity. She said again: 'Who can that be?'

I kept eating. It wouldn't be anyone to help me anyway. All I could think of was some way to escape from this mad couple's clutches. Nothing else mattered.

Uncle William came into the kitchen. 'Tourist,' he said. 'He's lost. Where's that map we had?' He began rummaging in one of the drawers.

Aunt Mary still peered out of the window. 'Sure? He looks more like a businessman to me.'

She suddenly realised I was still there. Her eyes flickered to me. 'We're not used to strangers round here, are we?'

I looked at her and smiled. *None stranger than you, Aunt Mary*, I thought.

'He's just looking for directions to the town,' Uncle William said. 'I'll get rid of him.' He found the map, snatched it up. 'Asked if we would be willing to put him up.'

I thought I would test him then. 'Why don't you? Make a bit of extra money. You've got a spare room.' But, I was thinking, with someone else here I'd be safe.

Aunt Mary shot me a look.

'Oh, no, we like it just to be our own little family, don't we?' She flashed one of those creepy smiles at me.

'Hurry up, Noel. We'll be late for school,' Uncle William said again as he went back outside.

I scooped up the last of my breakfast, and went into the hall to pull on my warm winter boots. Noel's boots. Aunt Mary came through carrying a flask of soup. 'Home-made lentil soup,' she told me. She pushed it into my rucksack, followed by a pack of sandwiches wrapped in cellophane. An apple completed my lunch. What were these people all about? Feeding me like this. Knowing I wasn't their nephew.

The front door lay open. I could hear Uncle William telling the tourist how to get to the nearest town. I could almost hear the man's murmured reply.

'Noel! We'll be late!' Uncle William called out to me.

I was ready to call back, but Aunt Mary did it for me. She hauled the door wide and shouted, 'He's just getting his boots on.' I watched as she flashed one of her smiles again at the tourist. 'Good morning. Terrible fog.'

There was no answer. I could almost imagine the man seeing that smile and wanting away from here as fast as possible.

At last I was ready. Aunt Mary shoved a chocolate bar into my hand. 'Just to keep you going.' She whispered it to me. Our secret. I stood up and stepped to the door.

Uncle William was still talking to the man, pointing down the road, giving directions to some invisible town, hidden in the fog.

The man began walking to his black car. He turned

slowly to say goodbye to Uncle William. I saw his face.

It was as if the world went into slow motion.

I saw his face.

His long face, his dark eyes.

The Dark Man.

20

WEDNESDAY

'I don't think we should be going to school.' Faisal thought he would give it one more try. 'The Beast could get us. It could leap right through the window of the school, snatch me up in its jaws.'

His dad only tutted. He looked up from his newspaper. 'Really, Faisal. You and that imagination of yours.'

He might have known his father wouldn't fall for it. His mother and his aunties and his granny – now, they were a different matter.

His mother came towards him, clutched him close to her. A small price to pay if she kept him off school. 'Oh, he is right, Father. We should keep him home with us where the Beast can't get him.'

His dad didn't even look up from his paper this time. 'Sit at the back of the class, Faisal. If the Beast gets in it will eat Kirsten and the new boy first. By the time it gets to you it won't be hungry.'

Auntie Munan moaned. 'How can you joke about such a thing?' She decided to hug him too.

'It's a beast you have married, sister,' Auntie Furzana joined in. 'Keep him off school. I will be his teacher.'

90

She beamed a smile at her favourite nephew. Faisal smiled back. Unfortunately that decided her to hug him too.

'Let him stay at home,' his granny urged. 'He can look after me. I need someone to cut my toenails.'

Faisal would even have done that for a day off school. His father was having none of it. He stood up. Put down his paper. He was taking his son to school. 'My dear, Faisal would do anything for a day off school. You know that. It wouldn't even surprise me if he had invented this Beast himself just so he would have an excuse for not going.'

'A body's been found. That's nothing to joke about,' his mother said.

It was a pity his dad wasn't away on business, like Kirsten's dad. Faisal's mum and his aunties, and his granny, would definitely have let him stay off school. Lolling around the house, watching television, eating chocolate, spoiled by them all.

His dad was suddenly more serious. 'I hope and pray that body is not the body of young Paul. But bodies have been found before. People who have stumbled into the mire, or got lost on the moors. Faisal is safer at school. Mr Darling will see no harm befalls him.'

Nothing else for it, Faisal thought. He would just have to go. Another boring day at school.

Kirsten's mother hadn't come in till the early hours of the morning. So much for one hour max! Where had she been? Kirsten was sure she had the answer at breakfast. Her mother had got up late, not like her at all, and came into the kitchen forcing a smile. Yes, she was definitely forcing it.

'Wonderful news, Kirsten. Your dad's coming home. Tomorrow. He phoned this morning.'

So that was why she'd stayed out so late. Her last night with her new boyfriend.

'Aren't you pleased?' her mother asked when she saw her frown.

And now it was Kirsten who forced a smile. 'Delighted.'

The man turned once again and shouted for this boy of his.

'Noel!'

He was eager to get off to school. Eager to get rid of *him* too. Something in that smile of his, he had too many teeth, told the Dark Man he wanted him away as soon as possible. Natural reticence for strangers? Or something else? Was he hiding something? The Dark Man saw mysteries everywhere.

'You don't know of a hotel near here? Even a bed and breakfast?'

'Sorry. We've only just moved here ourselves. Noel!' He called again into the house. 'My nephew – typical boy, eh? Have to drag him to school.'

'Do you work round here?'

'No, I gave up work for . . . health reasons. And you, is this just a holiday?'

'I have business here.'

92

He caught a glimpse of movement at the front door. The Dark Man turned slowly to look. He saw a flash of trousers, a red jacket, the heel of a shoe, the woman looking startled. 'Noel! What's wrong?'

The man was suddenly alert. 'What's wrong with Noel, Mary?'

'I think he's being sick, William.'

The man, William, turned back to him. 'I'll have to go. Noel hasn't looked well all morning. Hope you find something.'

The Dark Man stood for a moment, watching him. Then he got into his car and drove off.

I really did spew up. Wasn't faking it. Black spots swam in front of my eyes and I thought I was going to faint. It was as if I was zooming down a black tunnel, catching hints of words, sights of people. Flashing past me.

'*Run. Keep on running.*'

'*It's up to you.*'

'*Everything depends on you.*'

Someone's face, blurred, couldn't make out who it might be, but I could feel myself being shaken by the shoulders, ordered to do something I didn't understand. And I remembered being afraid.

Like I was afraid now.

The Dark Man had found me again – but how?

The body.

The body of a boy. My age. Unidentified.

It had been all over the news. He must think it was me. He hadn't wasted any time in getting here.

93

My hands were shaking. The Dark Man was here. After me. He had sworn he would get me, sworn he would be one step behind me, and he had found me again.

I stood in the bathroom with the door locked, while Aunt Mary pounded and called to me.

How could I escape him this time?

'Noel! Noel! Are you OK?'

The answer leapt at me as she called out my name. My name. Noel Christie.

How could I escape him this time? By being Noel Christie.

He suspected the dead boy was me. But even if he did ask if there were any strange boys in the area, there would be none. I, after all, was Noel Christie. Everyone, from the teacher to the other pupils, assumed that was who I was.

The Dark Man had come to the house, been metres from me, and hadn't been suspicious. Because I was the nephew of the house. Noel Christie.

I heard his car drive away. Aunt Mary knocked again on the door. 'Are you OK, Noel?' she asked again.

I muttered I was fine. Better now the Dark Man had gone.

I heard Uncle William hurry into the house. 'How is he?'

And Aunt Mary's answer. 'Maybe we can keep him off school now.'

I was about to answer, no, I was fine, when I heard just faintly Uncle William's whispered reply. 'No, Mary, you know we decided he had to go to school . . . for a few days at least.'

For a few days . . . at least. What were these two planning for me?

I had to get away from them . . . and yet, here, at least I was safe from the Dark Man . . . but then again, not safe at all.

My hands were shaking as I opened the toilet door. 'I think I ate too much breakfast,' I said. 'But I'm fine.'

Uncle William patted my shoulder. 'Course you are.'

As we drove to the school my eyes scanned the roads, the hills, looking everywhere for the Dark Man's black car. 'What did he want?' I asked.

'I think he's a reporter, no matter what he says. Too good a story to miss – body found on the moors. The place will be swarming with them soon.'

Was that good or bad for me? I didn't know. I didn't know anything.

All I knew was this wasn't fair. Once again, I was hemmed in, danger on every side.

21

Mr Darling looked at the three pupils in his class. Kirsten sat looking annoyed, or was that a worried frown? You could never tell with Kirsten. Her mother had a high-powered job. She was a scientist of some kind at the research facility. Never took any time off for Kirsten. Her father away on business. But he had been away quite a while. Mr Darling had wondered if perhaps he would ever come back, if the business trip wasn't actually a trial separation. But Mrs Stewart had told him today that her husband was returning. He was coming home tomorrow.

Faisal was never off school either, but for a different reason. His dad thought taking a day off school was a hanging offence.

And the boy, Noel. He sat staring at the floor, his sallow skin paler than ever.

He should have made the decision to close the school today. Why hadn't he? He'd thought all night about the body on the moors, and about Paul. He'd had to suffer his wife's icy reminders that they could have helped Paul more.

He'd heard a rumour that Paul's stepfather was being

questioned again by the police. They must be convinced the body was Paul's.

He must put these thoughts away. He was a teacher. 'So, we've had an exciting time since you arrived here, Noel,' he said pleasantly.

Kirsten answered, 'You call this exciting, sir? It's a tragedy.'

Why did she always have to be so troublesome, always ready for an argument?

'You don't have to worry now, anyway, Kirsten. Your mother was telling me that your dad is coming home tomorrow. Something for you to look forward to.'

She didn't look as if she was looking forward to it at all. She bit her bottom lip and turned away.

Uncle William had been right about the media. By mid morning a reporter and a photographer had arrived at the school. Two of them roared up in a Range Rover, jumped from the car and had pushed their way into the class before Mr Darling could stop them. 'You've no right to barge in here!' Mr Darling was out of his seat, rushing to the door, trying to force them out.

'We just want to interview a couple of the children who knew the dead boy.'

Faisal leapt to his feet. 'It's definitely Paul, then?'

The reported shrugged. 'Not confirmed, but the father's being held by the police. So not much doubt, eh?'

'I hope they throw away the key!' Faisal said angrily.

The reporter leapt on that. 'Tell us more. Why do you say that?'

'I will not have these children questioned. Get out of here.' Mr Darling silenced Faisal, could see he was ready to spill his guts.

'A photo then.' The photographer pushed forward, holding his camera high. 'You can't object to a photo.'

Kirsten said nothing. Faisal grinned, eager for publicity. It was me who yelled.

'No! I'm not allowed to have my photo taken.'

Did anyone else hear the panic in my voice? But a photograph published in a paper and the Dark Man would know then who Noel really was.

Kirsten swung round to me. 'Keep your hair on,' she said. 'Mr Darling's not going to allow a photo to be taken, are you, Mr Darling?'

'Indeed I am not!' Mr Darling held his arms wide, pushed them out of the door. They went reluctantly, still calling out to us for information.

Kirsten stared at me curiously. 'Why aren't you allowed to have your photo taken?' she asked.

I couldn't think of an answer. Luckily, good old Faisal provided one for me. 'Could be lots of reasons. Maybe his uncle and aunt adopted him, and his real parents want him back now.'

Even Kirsten gave me a reason. 'Maybe he's a killer on the run . . . and he's the one who's kidnapped his aunt and uncle.'

'My mystery,' was all I said.

'Sorry about that,' Mr Darling said to us when he came back in. He had waited till the Range Rover had wheelspun back on to the road before returning to the class.

'Sir, do you think it is Paul?' Faisal asked.

'I don't know.' He sounded weary.

'I think it is,' Faisal said.

Kirsten agreed. 'Who else could it be? What other boy that age has gone missing?'

A chill suddenly went through me, like someone walking over my grave.

What other boy had gone missing?

The dead body on the moors.

I was suddenly sure I knew who it might be.

The real Noel Christie.

22

Mysteries and secrets, Mr Darling was thinking. They all seemed to have them. Except perhaps Faisal. Like an open book, Faisal. But the new boy, Noel – almost panicking when the photographers came. Why? Had his aunt and uncle brought him here to get him away from abusive parents? They had been very secretive about their reasons for coming here. Noel had been seen by child psychologists. He needed careful looking after, they had told him. No one knew Noel was here. No one must know. He had thought it strange that the couple had chosen to come here in the first place, to this God forsaken place – desolate moorland with a beast roaming around. They had to be running away from something.

And now, Kirsten. Her father was coming home. Surely that should make her happy. Instead, she was sitting, biting her lip. Distracted. Worrying about something.

He looked out of the window. The fog was coming down again. Treacherous on the moors tonight.

Police cars zoomed past on the road all the morning.

But it wasn't police cars I was looking for. It was a black BMW. The Dark Man's car. He was here somewhere. What if he came to the school?

But why should he? He suspected I was the dead boy. He was here to find that out. Why should he bother with me? He thought I was Noel Christie. I was safe as long as he believed that. As long as he didn't see me.

Safe! What was I thinking about? I was living with a couple of homicidal maniacs who were pretending I was their nephew. Now I suspected that they had killed Noel. Was it his body that had been found on the moors?

They had killed him and needed someone to take his place, to prove he was still alive. For a while at least. Then I had come along, a boy on the run with nothing on him to identify him, with no memory. A perfect replacement.

But why did they need me?

My mind hurtled from one thing to another. What should I do? Run, or stay? Whatever I did, danger was all around me.

'Noel! Noel!'

I'd never get used to that name. I turned to the teacher. 'Sorry, sir.'

'What on earth is wrong with you all today? None of you are paying attention.' Mr Darling rapped the desk with his book.

Faisal beamed. 'I'm paying attention, Mr Darling.'

Kirsten only glared at him. For the first time I noticed how distracted she looked. As if she had the weight of the world on her shoulders.

The teacher told them all about the reporter and photographer when they came to collect the pupils at the end of the day. Faisal's father was annoyed. He took out a small leather notebook. 'Tell me which paper. I will contact them and complain. Coming to the school indeed!'

When he told Kirsten's mother she had remained glamorously blank. Her mind on other things. 'Is everything all right with Kirsten?' he asked her. 'She doesn't seem herself.'

She was flippant with her answer. 'She's just excited. Her dad's coming home.'

Excited nothing, Mr Darling thought. Worried, was more the word he would have used.

However, it was Noel's uncle's reaction that struck him most. Immediately, he had said, 'No photographs! I should have told you before. No photographs of Noel!'

'You don't have to worry,' the teacher had reassured him. 'Noel told me too, almost in as much of a panic about it as you are.'

Mr Darling waited for an answer. Waited for him to explain why he wouldn't allow his nephew's photograph to be taken. All he got was, 'There are reasons. I can't go into them now.'

Mr Darling watched the cars drive away. Secrets and mysteries, he thought again. He saw them everywhere.

Uncle William drove the boy home in silence. So he

102

didn't want his picture taken. Desperate not to have his picture taken, the teacher had said.

He had been right. No identification. No one looking for him. The boy had a secret too.

Better and better.

'I don't know why you're looking so miserable, Kirsten. I thought your dad coming home would cheer you up.'

All the way home Kirsten was silent, staring out at the passing landscape, deep in thought. Worrying about what was the right thing to do now.

'It does.' Kirsten tried to sound cheery. She hadn't thought her dad *was* coming home, ever again. She knew something had happened between her parents. She was sure now it had something to do with another man. She had missed her dad. And she couldn't have her mother getting suspicious. She could never trust her mum with her secret. Could she trust her dad? She dismissed that thought right away. No. She wouldn't trust anyone.

She was in a total muddle about what to do. If only there was someone she could rely on. Confide in. If only there was someone to help her.

Aunt Mary's beef goulash was delicious. Great slabs of bread to mop up the gravy. Sticky toffee pudding for dessert. They watched me eat with satisfaction.

'I love watching this nephew of ours enjoy his food,' Aunt Mary said.

I was worried sick, hadn't a clue what to do. But it

103

didn't spoil my appetite.

Aunt Mary came into my room before bedtime with hot chocolate for me.

'Why are you so good to me?' I asked her. I waited all the time for them to suddenly turn on me, yet all they did was smile and feed me.

'Because we love you, Noel.'

But I wasn't Noel, and they knew it. How long could I fool them that I believed it?

*

Kirsten lay in bed, staring at the ceiling. She had made her decision. There was only one thing she could do. She had done everything she possibly could have done. It couldn't go on any longer. She had to share it with someone. Tomorrow, it would be out of her hands.

*

Aunt Mary snuggled close to her husband. The boy was in bed. Another day over. For once her smile had disappeared. The stress of the whole situation was getting to her. 'This can't go on much longer.'

'It won't,' he assured her. 'Another couple of days, my dear, and it'll all be over.'

*

I lay in bed, staring at the ceiling. I couldn't sleep. I had to get away from here. But how? Tomorrow, I decided, I had to find some way to run.

23

THURSDAY

I woke up at midnight. Something was outside, prowling. I heard a lid knocked over. I leapt awake. My first thought, the Dark Man back to get me. I slipped out of bed, crossed to the window. I half expected Uncle William to bound into my room, thinking it was me, halfway out of the window. But there was not a sound in the house.

I peered out into the night. Darkness, like I'd never seen before. Pitch-black night. And then a movement, merging into the blackness. Sleek, black, silky movement in the night. Might not have been real. I blinked. Black against black, like a panther. But bigger. Much bigger. The word, the image snapped in my head. I remembered what a panther was. I pressed my face close to the glass. It was moving in the distance. Then I realised it had something in its jaws. Something large clenched tight in its jaws. A sheep. It was dragging it across the ground. I peered closer. Still couldn't make it out against the night. Yet it stopped, seemed to look up at me. I saw tiny dots of green light. I caught my breath, moved back into the shadow of my room. I was sure I could sense it still looking up at me.

I dared to look again. It was the sheep I saw, its limp head trailing on the ground. Then something seemed to shimmer in the shadows, and was gone, dragging the dead sheep with it. Gone so fast I might have imagined it.

I stared for a long time, watching in case it came back, desperate to see it again, yet terrified. It was hungry. It had come close for food, found a sheep on the moors. Now it had slipped away into the darkness again.

What had I seen? A black shadow, so black it merged into the night. Huge. Bigger than any ordinary beast. Not a puma, as they all thought, but something fiercer, more dangerous.

I had caught a glimpse of it.

And I couldn't tell a soul.

The body still hadn't been identified. Heard it on the radio next morning as I ate one of Aunt Mary's breakfasts.

'Goodness, that poor boy. How awful for his mother.'

'From what I've heard,' Uncle William said, 'she probably wouldn't care.' He peered over his paper at me. 'Ready, Noel?'

Why were they keeping this up? Why were they still pretending? I stood up. I could pretend too, for as long as I had to. 'I'm ready for anything.'

Kirsten had come to a decision in the night, made her plans. She'd done what she needed to do to set that plan into motion. By the time her mother came out of the house to take her to school. Kirsten was already waiting in the car.

'You're keen to go to school today,' her mother said.

She waited till her mother had started to drive, till they were well on the way before she said, 'Mum, I've got something to tell you.'

Her mother didn't glance her way. 'What, Kirsten?'

'I'd like you to speak to Mr Darling this morning.'

Her mother's face snapped round to her. All this was going to make her late for work, her only interest. 'I have an important meeting. Can't it wait?'

'No!' Kirsten snapped the words back at her. She could be as difficult as her mother. She watched her mother's knuckles tighten on the steering wheel.

'What's this about?'

'Faisal,' Kirsten said.

'Faisal? What about him?'

Kirsten took a deep breath. 'He's been bullying me for ages, and I want you to make him stop.'

'Faisal?' Her mother sounded more amazed than annoyed. 'Faisal's been bullying *you*?'

Kirsten was determined not to let it go. All part of her plan. 'Promise me when we get to school you'll talk to Mr Darling?'

Kirsten was late. Faisal and I watched her mother's big Jaguar roar up and park out of sight beside the bike shed. A moment later, her mother, all legs and hair, came striding into the school.

'She looks angry,' Faisal said. 'Probably couldn't find her mascara this morning.'

107

He was still grinning as the door was flung open and Kirsten's mother stood glaring at him.

Mr Darling stepped towards her. 'Something wrong, Mrs Stewart?'

'Something is very wrong!' she said at once. 'My daughter has just been telling me about the horrendous time this boy has been giving her!' She pointed an accusing long-nailed finger at Faisal.

He looked behind him. There was only blank wall. 'Me?' he said.

At the same time Mr Darling said in exactly the same amazed tone, 'Faisal?'

'Yes, Faisal. He's been bullying my Kirsten for ages.'

'I can hardly believe that Faisal . . .' Mr Darling didn't get another word out.

'Are you trying to say my daughter is a liar?'

'Well, of course not, but . . . Faisal?'

Faisal jumped to his feet. 'I did not. I've never bullied anybody!'

'Where is Kirsten?' Mr Darling asked.

For the first time she seemed to notice her daughter wasn't with her. 'Probably too frightened to come in and face him!'

Now that didn't sound like Kirsten at all, even to me, who had only known her for a few days.

Just then Kirsten came into the classroom. Her face was red, she looked sheepish. And so she should. Calling Faisal a bully? And bullying Kirsten of all people.

I'd only just met her and knew already she was not a person who could be bullied.

'Is this true?'

Faisal answered the question. 'No, it is not!' He turned to me. 'You back me up, Noel. I don't bully her, do I?'

'How would he know?' Kirsten snapped out. 'He's only been in the school a couple of days.'

'Why haven't you mentioned anything about this before, Kirsten?' Mr Darling said.

That only made Kirsten's mother even more angry. 'There you go again. Talking as if you don't believe her.'

'That's the reason I haven't said anything.' Kirsten sniffed, as if she was about to cry. 'I knew you wouldn't believe me, Mr Darling.'

Kirsten could think fast, I had to give her that. But why? Why was she lying about this?

Mrs Stewart glanced at her watch. All this was keeping her back. Mr Darling saw it too. 'Leave this with me. I can assure you that your daughter won't be bullied again.'

Kirsten's mother let out a long sigh. 'I'm so glad her father's home tomorrow. It's very difficult for a woman on her own.' She checked her watch again. 'I really will have to go. Important meeting.' As she turned she glared at Faisal. I saw Faisal swallow. It took all his courage not to step back. Mr Darling saw her out.

Just enough time for Faisal to snap at Kirsten, 'What's your game? You're getting me into big trouble.'

Just enough time for me to ask, 'Why are you lying, Kirsten?'

Just enough time for Kirsten to reply, 'I'll explain it all later, at break, and then you'll understand everything.'

24

Had he been wrong? Everyone here in this small town seemed to be of the same opinion. The body on the moors was some local boy, badly treated by his step-father, always running away. Even though there was still no positive identification, no one seemed to have any doubt who the body was.

Was he wasting his time here? Letting his real prey get further away from him? And time was running out. But he had to be sure. Some instinct was telling him that the boy was close. Alive or dead.

So he would wait. Meanwhile he had to find some-where to stay. The only hotel had been taken up by reporters from city newspapers. And he had already spent one uncomfortably cold night driving. He needed to rest.

He pulled into a garage at the edge of the small town to fill up. As he paid for his petrol he asked the assistant, 'Anywhere else around here I could stay besides the hotel?'

The girl behind the counter took his money absently. 'I think the school teacher's wife takes in boarders. That's in the summer usually, but she might make an exception in these circumstances.' She suddenly looked interested in him. 'Are you a reporter?' She pushed her hair back hopefully. When he told her he wasn't a reporter the old bored look settled on her face again. 'I'd try the school then.'

He would call the schoolhouse first. Try his luck there. There was no way he was sleeping in a car tonight.

'I'm going to kill her at break!' Faisal whispered to me.

'And prove her right,' I warned him.

'I don't care. Mr Darling's going to tell my dad. My dad'll go spare. Me, a bully? It's Kirsten who's the bully.'

I had to agree with that. What was Kirsten up to?

Mr Darling had given them both a talking to. As soon as Kirsten's mother had left he had taken them both to his desk and talked to them softly, but firmly. I could see from his face he didn't believe Kirsten, but like me, he didn't understand why she should say such a thing. What was going on in that devious brain of hers?

Anyway, I had my own problems. I had to get away from here and I didn't know how. Today, there was an even heavier police presence on the roads. Cars speeding by constantly. Mr Darling told us that armed police had been brought in.

No more talk of sedation. Now, they were out to kill. I had seen this Beast, glimpsed its shiny black fur. I couldn't tell anyone. Couldn't risk any kind of publicity.

Yet, I had seen it. No one else but me.

Well, no one alive, I remembered, thinking of the

body on the moors.

It was still morning when the door of the classroom opened and Mrs Darling popped her head round. Her face was pale, her eyes sad. They'd lost a child, Faisal had said, and she'd never quite got over it.

'Sorry to disturb you.' Her eyes skimmed over us apologetically. As if we minded. She looked back to her husband. 'Can I speak to you, dear?' She beckoned her husband out of the room.

He turned to us. 'I want no fighting while I'm out of here. Right?! Get your books out and study the war.'

I almost smiled at that. Study a war! Just the thing to make you want peace.

As soon as he pulled the door closed Faisal turned on Kirsten. 'You'd better spill the beans right now.'

'Spill the beans!' Kirsten tutted. 'Are you listening to yourself?' She glanced out of the window. Mr Darling was going into the back door of his house. 'He could be back at any minute. No time. You'll just have to wait.' She suddenly drew in her breath. 'I don't even know if I'm doing the right thing trusting you – trusting either of you.'

It seemed to me like she was talking to herself. Arguing with herself. I could see the signs. I did it all the time. I was even more intrigued.

'You can wait till break, can't you?' Then she turned away and wouldn't even look at us.

'What is going on?' Faisal asked me.

'I know as much as you.' I shrugged. 'She probably just wants attention from her mother. She doesn't seem to get any.'

'I wish I knew her secret,' Faisal said.

One thing for sure, I thought, it would be nothing like mine.

25

'He sounded like a gentleman,' Millie was saying. 'He only needs a room for a couple of nights.'

'You're sure he's not a reporter?' That was the last thing Mr Darling needed here.

'He doesn't seem interested in the school. He says he's a businessman. Do you think we should let him stay?'

She always needed his approval now. How he wished he could have back the woman he married. Sure of herself, confident, fun. All that had gone. Depression and resentment had taken their place. He was happy for anything that would take her mind off the past. 'You're sure it won't be too much trouble for you?'

'No. It will give me something to do. He's calling back in ten minutes. I can tell him yes, then?'

'Tell him yes,' Mr Darling said.

'You always have the best stuff to eat, Noel.' Faisal looked longingly at my lunchbox, Kirsten forgotten for a moment. 'Your Aunt Mary's a great cook. Can I adopt her?'

Have her with my pleasure, I wanted to say and for a

second, a split second, I almost confided in Faisal. Almost told him that I didn't know who I was, but I wasn't this Noel.

The moment passed. Mr Darling gathered up his papers, tapped the desk. It was break time at last. Secret time.

'Now during break, I don't want any of you causing any trouble.' His words were directed at Faisal and Kirsten.

'Don't look at me, sir! I never cause any trouble.' Faisal glared at Kirsten. 'She's the one causing the trouble.'

'Any more of that talk and you won't get a break,' Mr Darling warned and that was enough to keep us quiet. He looked at Kirsten. 'Of course, you can come with me and have your break at the house, Kirsten.'

Faisal nearly burst then. He was desperate to find out what she was up to. He broke in. 'I promise, sir, I'll be on my best behaviour.'

Kirsten smirked. 'I'll be fine, sir.'

As soon as he was out of the room Faisal jumped to his feet. 'Right, missy, what's your game?'

Kirsten stood up. For the first time since I'd known her she looked vulnerable. Her eyes welled up, but she sniffed and the tears were gone.

'What you're going to see is a secret. A secret you'll never tell. You have to promise me that, hand on heart. You won't tell. You'll never tell. I'll never forgive either of you if you tell.'

'I know how to keep a secret,' Faisal said.

Her eyes moved to me. 'I don't even know you.'

'I know,' I said. 'But I promise, you can trust me too.'
She took a deep breath. 'Come with me.'

Mr Darling wanted to meet this 'businessman', wanted to reassure himself that he wasn't a reporter, just here for a story. The man was already in the house when he went in to the kitchen. That surprised him. He hadn't heard the car on the drive. He could have missed seeing it, of course. The man had obviously taken the driveway that led to the house and had parked at the front, out of sight of the school.

He was having a cup of tea in their kitchen. A slim dark man, sitting comfortably at the table, eating gingernuts.

'This is Mr McGuffin,' his wife said.

Mr McGuffin stood up. He didn't look like a reporter. He looked severe, too well dressed. But still, the teacher was wary.

'What brings you to this part of the world? Business with the research facility?'

He was annoyed at himself for answering his own question.

'Yes,' Mr McGuffin said. 'Seems I picked an exciting time to come – a beast on the loose and a body on the moors.'

Mr Darling nodded.

'One of your pupils, your wife was saying.'

'We don't know that for sure, yet,' Mr Darling said.

'Let's hope it's not him,' Mr McGuffin said, meaning every word.

Kirsten led us out of the back door of the schoolhouse, across the covered walkway, out of sight of the house, and towards the bike shed. She stood for a moment with her hand on the door. I could see that hand shaking. She turned to us one more time. 'Please, promise. I have to know I can trust you.'

She sounded so serious, as if life depended on it. Even Faisal was impressed.

I reached out and touched her shaking hand. 'We promise, Kirsten. What are you so afraid of?' Because she was afraid, and I knew fear.

She pushed the door open silently, and let the light in. Faisal and I stepped inside. The shed looked empty. Hardly ever used now, I imagined, except perhaps in summer when pupils had come to school on their bikes, in the days before the Beast.

Then, I caught a movement in the corner. I stepped back, tried to see the shape in the dim light.

There, crouched on the floor, was a boy. I began to make out his face. He stared back at us boldly.

Faisal gasped beside me.

'Who is it?' I asked.

It seemed an age before Faisal answered.

'It's Paul.'

26

The boy in the corner. Paul Wilkie? No wonder Faisal was surprised. The boy, Paul, got to his feet, stepped forward. He held out his hands to Kirsten. 'Did you bring anything to eat?'

Kirsten put her hands on her hips. 'That's all he goes on about. Food, food, food. He's been driving me up the wall.'

She threw a packet of crisps at him. He caught it like an expert, grinned.

For once in his life Faisal was literally lost for words. He stared at Paul, then turned back to Kirsten. 'You've been hiding Paul all this time?'

'And it's been absolute murder. He's been in our garage.'

Paul snapped back at her. 'And let me tell you it was blinking cold in there.'

Kirsten looked shocked. 'I don't believe you! You're so ungrateful. Where else could I hide you? I couldn't bring you into the house, could I?' She looked at me and Faisal. 'I let him sleep in the car at night, plenty of blankets, plenty of food. Don't listen to him when he says he was cold and hungry.'

'Why did you bring him here?' I asked.

'My dad's coming home. My mum just parks the car in the garage and forgets about it till the morning. But my dad, he works about in the garage, he's always in and out of there. And he's coming home tomorrow. I didn't know what to do with him. I had to take him somewhere.'

Paul spluttered crisps all over the place. 'You're talking about me as if I'm a parcel.'

Faisal was still gobsmacked. He was staring at Kirsten, his mouth hanging open.

'Are you trying to catch flies or something?' she asked.

'You've been hiding Paul?' he said again, as if he was trying to take it in.

Kirsten took a step closer to him. 'Why should that be such a surprise? Because I'm a girl?'

'No,' Faisal said. 'Because you're you.'

She tutted. 'Just because I read girlie magazines and like fashion, don't think I'm not made of steel. You know the saying, a woman's like a tea bag. You don't know how strong she is until you put her in hot water.'

'I've never heard that saying in my life. Have you, Noel?'

I wanted to tell him I'd hadn't heard any old saying, but I could understand why he was amazed. I was amazed too. Amazed and impressed. Kirsten had been hiding Paul!

'So how did it all come about?' I asked her.

'Helloooo!' Paul waved his hands. 'I'm here. You can ask me.' He came closer. He was as tall as me, but much thinner. His eyes looked as if they didn't trust anyone. 'I ran away again, and this time I was determined that no one was going to bring me back. Rather take my chances with that Beast or the mire.'

'I found him at my place. He was trying to steal a blanket.'

'Borrow, Kirsten. Borrow.'

'Whatever!' she said. 'It was just at the time the Beast had been first sighted. We'd had letters home warning us about it. I couldn't let him go out on the moors. My dad was away. I knew he'd be safe in the garage.' She looked from me to Faisal. 'Somebody had to help him.'

'Good for you, Kirsten,' I said. I was looking at her with new eyes.

'So what's all this got to do with you telling your mother I bully you?'

'I had to get mum out of the car this morning and into the school. You know she never does that. She drops me off and she's away. She hardly gives me a chance to close the door. She usually drives off with my leg still in the car. I needed a direction to get Paul out of the boot.'

'Diversion,' Faisal corrected. Kirsten glared at him.

'And the boot of a car is not the most comfortable place in the world, I might add,' Paul said.

Kirsten turned on him. 'Oh, shut up, you!' She turned back to us. 'As soon as Mum was in the school yapping at Mr Darling, I had Paul out of the boot and in here.'

I began to laugh, couldn't help it. They all looked at me. 'Well, come on. The whole place has been cordoned off. Police everywhere searching for Paul, and Kirsten's got him in her garage all the time. Brilliant!'

Kirsten beamed. 'Somebody had to help him. If they found him, they'd only send him back with some feeble excuse that they'd monitor the situation.'

'They say that all the time,' Paul said. 'Social worker comes in a few times, Wilkie tells him or her I'm out, or I'm sleeping, and they believe him, don't bother to come back for weeks. Or we move again – new school, new social workers – then they say we've been lost in the system, same old story, just new bruises.' He sounded bitter and angry, and I didn't blame him.

'I'm not going back.' He looked at each of us, daring us to disagree.

'I won't let you,' Kirsten said. 'I just don't know what to do with you now.'

Faisal said suddenly, 'Mr Darling would help us.'

The three of us said almost at the same time, 'No!'

'But Mr Darling's a really nice man. You like him, Paul. He was always trying to help you.'

'Oh yeah, he's a really nice man. A nice law-abiding man. He'll do the right thing – within the law. He'll contact the authorities. That's what he did before . . . No way.' Paul suddenly moved back defensively as if he thought we might make a run at him and force him to Mr Darling's door.

'Paul's right,' I said. 'We can't trust an adult to help. Any adult. Their best intentions won't help Paul. We have to figure this out for ourselves.'

'I hoped you'd say that.' Kirsten looked at me closely. 'I didn't think I could trust you.'

'But where are we going to hide him now?' asked Faisal. 'He can't stay here.'

'I don't know the answer to that,' I said. 'Not yet. We'll have to think about it.'

Faisal went on excitedly. 'I mean, the police are everywhere. And there's a wild beast on the loose. And a body's been found on the moor.' Suddenly, he gasped, grabbed his head with both hands. 'The body on the moor! It's not Paul after all!'

'I wondered when you would figure that one out,' Kirsten said. 'That's why I was so shocked when Mr Darling told us about it. Then I thought, it might work for Paul. I mean, no one will be looking for him now. We can get him away. But . . . the body of a boy . . . his age . . . If it isn't Paul, who on earth can it be?'

There was a long silence. 'I think it might be me,' I said.

27

'Perhaps you'd like to say hello to the pupils?' Mr Darling suggested. Break was over. He needed to get back. 'I don't want them thinking there's a complete stranger lurking about.'

The man, Mr McGuffin, stood up. 'If you'd like me to. Although they won't see much of me. I'll probably be on my way tomorrow.'

'I know. I just like to keep them informed, especially now, with Paul disappearing and a body found on the moors and this wild animal roaming about,' he went on. 'I don't want it to be Paul, but who else could it be? Hardly likely another boy his age could be missing round these parts.'

Millie dropped a cup and it smashed on the floor. 'Don't say that. I can't bear to think it's Paul.'

He glanced from his wife to Mr McGuffin. 'Come on, then, they'll be finished with their break. I only have three pupils. Faisal, what a boy! Never stops talking. Kirsten, her mother works in the research facility nearby, very clever woman – maybe you've met her? And our new boy, Noel Christie.'

'Yes, I was at his house earlier. Met the uncle.'

Mr Darling could have said more, about Noel always running away, about the weird smiles of this Uncle William and Aunt Mary, but that would only be gossip. All he said was, 'Finished your coffee? Shall we go?'

'Poor Paul,' Millie said, almost as if she was talking to herself. 'He had a horrible life. No one to help him. Some people don't deserve children.'

Mr McGuffin paused, looked at her, as if he was waiting for her to say more. Mr Darling was afraid all her bitterness would flood out, and in front of a complete stranger. He just wanted McGuffin away from Millie.

As they walked towards the classroom, Mr Darling explained. 'I'm sorry about that. This business with Paul has affected her quite a lot. We lost a child. Broke Millie's heart.' Why was he telling him this? Because he had no one else to tell? Or because all this had affected him as much as Millie? 'She would have adopted Paul if they'd let her. She would have stolen him if I'd let her.'

'I understand,' Mr McGuffin said.

The teacher stopped at the door of the school. 'You've lost a child too?'

The man nodded. 'A boy.'

'You never get over it, do you?' Mr Darling said.

'No, I keep expecting that I'll just open a door and see him standing there.'

And Mr Darling opened the door.

The classroom was empty. *Typical children*, the Dark Man thought, *never obeying orders*. The teacher, who looked as if he was always a gentle man, was annoyed.

124

Natural, he supposed. There was a wild beast on the loose. He'd be the one in trouble if anything was to happen to his pupils.

'Faisal! Kirsten! Noel!' He turned to the Dark Man. 'You leave them for a moment and they take the first opportunity to disobey you.'

The Dark Man was glad. He had no desire to meet these children. None of them was the one he was searching for. He glanced at his watch. He wanted to get back into the small town, find out if the body had been identified yet. He couldn't risk wasting any more time here if the body was that of this Paul.

'Maybe I could meet them another time,' he said. 'But I have an appointment and I don't want to be late.'

'Of course,' Mr Darling said, and saw him to the door. Suddenly Faisal practically fell into the classroom through the back door. 'Sorry, sir, we were exploring the bike shed. We weren't outside, honest.' He pointed back through the door to the covered walkway.

'You know I asked you to stay in here.'

'Sorry, sir.' He looked back into the bike shed, shouted, 'Come on! Mr Darling's waiting!'

'I'll just be going.' The Dark Man was anxious now to be away. He hadn't time to listen to this teacher giving his pupils a telling-off.

'Of course. This is Faisal, by the way.'

'Hello, Faisal.'

'Mr McGuffin will be staying at my house, perhaps for a couple of days.'

Suddenly, a girl appeared. A little flushed, worried looking, probably expecting trouble from her teacher.

'Sorry, sir,' she said.

'Say hello to Mr McGuffin, Kirsten.'

Kirsten managed to force a smile.

'I really have to go.' The Dark Man would wait no longer.

The teacher opened the door of the classroom and the Dark Man left.

And Ram ran in through the other door.

28

'Mr Darling brought a friend of his in here to meet us,' Faisal whispered. 'Mr McGuffin his name is. He's staying with him just now.'

I wasn't interested in Mr Darling's friend. I had too much to think about. The body on the moors wasn't Paul. Therefore, the body on the moors might just be the real Noel Christie.

He'd run away. Let's face it, who wouldn't run away from Uncle William and Aunt Mary?

For some reason they needed a replacement – I didn't know why – hadn't figured that out yet. And along I came. A boy, the same age as their nephew with no identification, and even better, no memory.

How convenient for them that I came along that night. They'd probably searched my pockets, found nothing in Jake's coat. No identification. Probably redialled the number I'd called. They knew all the time I was lying. So I became Noel. And they almost convinced me. If it hadn't been for that photograph, maybe I would still think I was Noel too.

No doubt in my mind now.

The body on the moors was the real Noel.

I had to get away from here!

Mr Darling turned to the blackboard. Faisal leant across to me. His usually bright eyes were full of worry. 'What did you mean about the body being you?' he whispered.

'I'll tell you at lunch,' I whispered back. I was going to tell them everything. They deserved to know. Kirsten especially had proved her worth.

Mr Darling turned back to face us. His face was grim. 'Now why did you leave here when I told you especially not to?'

'Me and Faisal wanted to talk,' Kirsten said at once. Boy, she was a good liar. 'We've made up, sir. And it's all thanks to Noel here. He was brilliant. He was like the devil's advocaat.'

Mr Darling couldn't hide a smile. 'I think you mean the devil's advocate, Kirsten. But I'm glad you've made up. Now, let's get back to some lessons.'

It was hardly worth his while staying here. He was following a bad lead – losing time. The body had to be this Paul – everyone thought so. And anyway, hadn't he been told to move on? He reread the email that had appeared on his phone just moments ago:

Boy. Right age. Seen in Birmingham. Go.

What could he do?

He'd had a gut feeling about this. For once his gut feeling seemed to have let him down.

He parked the car and made his way to the police station. A tumble of reporters came rushing out.

Something was happening. His nerves tensed. He began to quicken his pace. He grabbed one of the reporters by the shoulders as he ran past him. 'What's happened?'

The man pulled away from him, kept running. 'The body on the moors – it wasn't that local boy at all. They've just released Wilkie, the stepfather.'

He had only reached the door of the station when a man, thin as a wire, stumbled through. He had lank fair hair – a lock of it fell across his face. He swept it back angrily. The Dark Man had never seen anyone so angry. He pushed everyone aside, all the reporters, except for one. He was from one of the tabloids, the name of his paper emblazoned on the T-shirt under his jacket.

'I'll sell you my story,' this man, Wilkie, rasped. 'See the cops, I'm gonny make them sorry. I'm gonny sue them, sue somebody. Wrongful arrest. Somebody's gonny pay for this.'

The Dark Man stepped aside, let the angry man pass.

His pulse raced. The body was not that of the local boy. He flicked open his phone, emailed an answer. He was staying. But he wasn't wasting any more time. He was going to have a look at this body for himself.

Uncle William and Aunt Mary listened intently to the news on the radio.

'So, it wasn't this Paul,' Aunt Mary said.

'No,' answered Uncle William. 'I never really thought it was, did you?'

'Of course not. I mean, it's hardly likely there would be two boys' bodies up there.'

It was just before lunch when Millie came rushing into the classroom. Her husband was surprised to see her. She seldom came to the classroom. Her face was flushed, her eyes bright. 'There's just been a newsflash on the radio. The body on the moors. It isn't Paul.' She glanced round at them. 'It's not your friend.'

He looked at them too, expecting jubilation. Maybe even a bit of cheering. What kind of children were they? They showed no reaction at all. They looked blank. Kirsten stared at her desk. The new boy, Noel, bit his lip. Only Faisal showed any emotion. 'That's good news, sir.' But with no conviction whatsoever.

'We can only hope that Paul is far away from here,' Mr Darling told them. 'If he's managed to get out of the area, he's probably safe somewhere. Maybe he's found a half-decent relative who'll look after him.'

'Would they let him stay with another relative, sir?' It was Noel who asked. 'Or would they send him back?'

How could he answer that? 'I'm sure they would take Paul's best interests into consideration,' he said.

'And then send him back,' Kirsten snapped out.

'What if his mother insisted he come back?' Faisal asked.

Faisal knew that was what had happened before, when Mr Darling and his wife had offered, begged, to keep him with them. His mother had insisted on her rights as a mother, and Paul had gone back. That had been the last time.

It was his wife who answered. 'You see, children

130

understand so much more than so-called sensible adults.'

She said it bitterly, remembering, he knew, how often they had tried to protect Paul, keep him safe. His mother had always been the stumbling block. Millie always made him feel so guilty, but what could he have done? He drew in a deep breath. 'I think it's wonderful news. Paul is alive and far away from here.'

His wife looked ready to cry. She turned and stormed from the room as if he had done something wrong. He wanted to follow her, but he wouldn't. None of it was his fault.

29

It was this war we were studying again. I tried to concentrate on it, but there was so much killing. Millions upon millions died. Why couldn't I remember hearing about it before? You would think so much death would stick in my memory. It had happened long before my time, but surely this was the kind of thing, once heard of, you would never forget?

Hitler. Winston Churchill. Roosevelt. Stalin. How could I have forgotten powerful names like those?

But the killing, the dying. It stunned me there could be so much cruelty in the world.

I was glad good won in the end. Hoped that was the way it would always be. There could never be such evil in the world again, surely.

Yet there was courage too. Heroes and heroines.

'Never in the field of human conflict has so much been owed by so many to so few.' One of Churchill's most famous sayings, Mr Darling told us. I heard it for the first time and was impressed.

The 'few' – the men in the air force who had saved the country from invasion. And the Resistance too, in all these occupied countries, willing to risk their lives to save Allied airmen, to hide them, protect them, take them to somewhere safe.

Suddenly, in the middle of the lesson, the classroom door was flung open. A thin fair-haired man burst into the class. He looked as if he had run all the way here, breathless and angry. We certainly hadn't heard a car. I didn't recognise him, but Faisal did. So did Kirsten. So did Mr Darling.

'Get out of this school, Mr Wilkie.'

Faisal looked at me. 'The stepfather,' he mouthed.

I looked again at Wilkie. I could see now the cruel line of his mouth, his body taut like a steel cable. He sprung at the teacher. I'd never seen a man so angry. 'You know where he is, don't you? You've been hiding him!'

Mr Darling swallowed. He was afraid. I could see the fear in him and I didn't blame him one bit. I'd never seen such violent anger as I saw in this Wilkie.

'Get out of here. Now!' Mr Darling said.

'You tell that waste of space that he's gonny be sorry when I get him. He thought he got a hammerin' before . . . but I'll snap him in two when I get my hands on him this time.'

I cowered from the viciousness in the threat. I imagined Paul, hiding in the shed. Could he hear? Bet he could. How terrified he must feel. How scared. Was this what they had sent him back to, time and again? Shrinking back from this man's fists, but never far enough.

Mr Darling began pushing Wilkie out of the door.

'Get your paws off me!'

'We'll discuss this outside, Mr Wilkie.' He was still trying to keep the peace, edging Paul's stepfather towards the door. Wilkie pushed him back so he stumbled against the wall, but he kept his feet. Mr Darling was determined to get him out of the classroom, determined to protect us.

As soon as the teacher had him outside the door he pulled it shut behind him. Kirsten and Faisal were on their feet instantly, running to the window. I saw Mrs Darling at her kitchen door; she was on the phone, calling the police probably. Wilkie was pushing at Mr Darling, his anger oozing from him.

Kirsten suddenly turned to me. 'I'm never sending him back to that!'

Faisal joined in. 'Me, neither.'

The words he had said still chilled me: *I'll snap him in two*.

'We're not going to,' I said. An idea was running through my mind, growing, exciting me. Why not? Why couldn't it work? It could. We could make it work.

'I know exactly how we're going to help Paul.'

30

The body was being kept in a funeral home in the town. Easy to find that out. In a small place like this people were always ready to talk about such an exciting development. They knew all the gossip. And were always happy to share it.

'The local police station's the size of a phone box. Nowhere to keep a body there,' the man in the newsagent had informed him.

'Got to put him somewhere cold . . . you know.' This from some old biddy waiting at a bus stop.

'Mr Dyer, the undertaker, is awful obliging. We get bodies here that often, from the moors, climbers, walkers and that. They're usually sent on to the nearest police mortuary, but with this being a local boy . . .'

And with that the eyes of the woman in the post office had filled up with genuine grief. 'The wee laddie would have to be kept here for identification.'

But the 'wee laddie' was no longer a local boy. So his body would soon be transported to the city. He had to see it before then, assure himself it was the boy he was after. Had to be. Too much of a coincidence if it wasn't.

He had gone to a secluded spot across the street from

the undertaker's, watched from a safe distance the comings and the goings; watched as the door was locked for a late lunchtime, and the place left empty.

No time to lose. He sprinted across the street. He could open any door, disarm any alarm. He had been well taught.

'I wish we could go and see how Paul is. Do you think he heard?' Kirsten was at the window, watching for the teacher. He was still outside, arguing with Wilkie, keeping him at bay till the police arrived.

'You can't risk going to Paul,' I told Kirsten. 'You can't risk leading that beast to him. You've kept him safe for too long.'

Kirsten nodded. 'I know.' She glanced back at the window. 'Right! You've got some explaining to do. The body on the moors is you! What's all that about?'

This morning I wouldn't have trusted either of them with my secret, but I had seen a side to Kirsten I really admired. And if I told her, I would have to trust Faisal too. But then they were trusting me with Paul.

'I'm not Noel Christie,' I said.

Faisal's head swivelled round so fast I thought it would spin across the room. Kirsten's eyes narrowed suspiciously.

'Have you ever met Noel Christie?' I asked.

'No,' Kirsten said. 'You were supposed to start school two weeks ago.'

'And you'd run away,' added Faisal.

'So how do you know I'm Noel Christie?'

136

'Because your uncle brought you here and introduced you as Noel Christie.' I could see that Kirsten was beginning to understand. 'But why would he lie?'

So I told them everything. Everything I knew at least. Mr Nobody whose memory only began two weeks ago. I told them about waking up in a tower block and finding a dying man in the lift; I told them about Gaby and Zoe and Jake; I told them all that had happened in that riverside town, about the Dark Man, who was after me because of a secret I had locked in my memory. The man who was still after me. I told them how I was picked up on the moors by Uncle William.

'How do you know you aren't this Noel, if you can't remember everything?' Kirsten wanted to know. Sensible question. Hadn't I begun to suspect I was Noel too?

'I found his photo,' I said, 'in a box in the loft. I think the body on the moors is the real Noel. I think Uncle William and Aunt Mary murdered him.'

They didn't argue with that. 'Makes sense,' Kirsten said. 'They needed you as a substitute . . . but why?'

'I don't know. But there has to be a reason. They need it to look as if Noel Christie's still alive. I just don't know for how long.'

'That's why you didn't know who Elvis was? Or who won the war?' Kirsten said. 'I thought you were just thick.'

'Thanks.'

'I don't understand how you can remember some things . . . and not others,' Faisal wanted to know. 'Like, you can't remember where you came from, who you are.

You didn't even remember about the war, about men landing on the moon. But you can still remember how to read and write . . . can't you?'

I didn't understand that either. 'I've never studied amnesia. I don't know how it's supposed to work.'

'So, can you remember your real name?' Kirsten asked me.

I shook my head. 'I made up the name.' Now I spoke it for the first time since I came here. 'Ram. I called myself Ram. Don't know where it came from?'

Faisal smiled. 'It suits you,'

'It suits me! I made it up, Faisal.'

'No, I mean it. Ram. Don't you understand what it means?'

I didn't know what he was talking about.

'Ram,' he said. 'R.A.M. Random Access Memory. Computer talk. That's what you've got. Random access to your memory.'

There were coffins of every description, coffins of pale white wood, coffins of mahogany, coffins of polished pine. Some lay with open lids, displaying the luxury within – quilted velvets, silks of every colour. The traffic sounds outside were muted as he padded through the quiet gloom of the coffin room. He moved silently into the next chamber. The coffin in here wasn't empty. An old man lay there, snug in blue silk, his face impassive, his mouth set. He might have only been sleeping. Peaceful in death. He almost expected the old man's eyes to snap open, stare back at him.

He wasn't afraid. There was nothing to fear in death. It was the living he was afraid of. The boy, if he was still alive. The boy and what he knew. What he might remember. He had to find him.

He trod silently into the next chamber. This was more like it. Here there were steel drawers for holding the dead. He read each white card on the front, displaying the name of the occupant of each drawer. At last he found the one he was looking for.

Boy. Identity Unknown.

He clasped his hands round the handle and pulled softly. The drawer slid open.

Perhaps another man would have gasped at the sight before him. The state of the boy's body, of his face. The Beast on the moors had certainly got him.

The Dark Man was neither sick, nor disgusted. He only knew his search was not over.

Because even without a face he knew this was not the boy he was after. The hands were the giveaway. He knew the boy well enough to know these weren't his hands. Hadn't he shown him how to fold them round a rifle?

The boy was still alive.

31

'So, Mr Nobody, what's your brilliant idea for helping Paul?!' It was all Kirsten was really interested in, helping Paul.

I checked to make sure Mr Darling was still out there. Wilkie was still pushing at him, spoiling for a fight. I was sure in a moment Mr Darling would lose it altogether.

'The Resistance,' I said.

They both looked at me blankly.

'The Resistance during the Second World War,' I explained. 'They passed airmen and soldiers from one group to another until they reached safety. That's what we're going to do with Paul.'

'How?' Kirsten asked. 'How do we pass him on to anybody? We're practically under police protection now.'

'Do you think that stopped the Resistance?' I asked her. 'And I mean, we're hardly likely to get shot at dawn if we're caught.'

'And who are we going to pass him on to?' Faisal wanted to know.

'I can't think of everything.' I was beginning to get annoyed. They were turning my bright idea into a farce

. . . or maybe just letting me see the flaws in it. 'Haven't you got anybody in your family you could trust?'

'My cousin Abdullah,' Faisal said at once. 'He's my best friend too. We text each other all the time. We're always exchanging computer games – the ones you're not supposed to watch. He sneaks them to me in his van when he comes on a Friday. We call it our special delivery.'

'Is he an adult?' I wasn't sure we should trust any adult with this.

'He's seventeen, going on twelve. He's as daft as Faisal,' Kirsten said.

'My cousin's brilliant!' Faisal snapped at her. 'He's seventeen and he's got his own business already.'

Kirsten sniffed. 'Thinks he's an entrypenure.'

'It's entrepreneur. And if you want to know, he's going to be a millionaire!'

'Enough!' I almost shouted. 'Can you trust him, Faisal?'

'If he's anything like you, I wouldn't trust him,' Kirsten said.

Faisal snapped back at her. 'Have you got anybody you can trust? Oh no, I keep forgetting. You've not got any friends.'

'She's the one who was brave enough to look after Paul,' I reminded Faisal. 'Are you sure you can trust your cousin?'

'With my life,' he said immediately.

'It's Paul's life we're talking about,' Kirsten said.

Faisal slammed his fist down on the desk. 'I've just had a brilliant idea. Abdullah comes here every Friday.

He delivers Mrs Darling's shopping. I'll tell Abdullah we've got a special delivery for him. Tomorrow, we sneak Paul into the back of the van, he hides there, Abdullah gets him out and passes him on.' He snapped his fingers. 'Paul's gone.'

'Passes him on to who?' I asked.

'To other people we can trust,' Faisal said.

'Would it really work?' Kirsten said hopefully.

'Why not?' I said, and already another plan was forming in my head. Why hadn't I thought of it before? Because if Paul could escape that way, so could I.

'I have to check on Paul,' Kirsten said. For the first time I saw her as a mother hen. She had saved Paul. She'd been looking after him all this time. This morning I couldn't stand her. Yet now? She was somebody I really admired.

Mr Darling was still out there with Wilkie. Still trying to talk to him, reason with him. He didn't understand that there are some people you just can't reason with.

There was no point in trying to stop Kirsten. 'You do that, then,' I said. 'We'll watch out for any trouble.'

Faisal waited till she'd gone. 'Who'd have believed it, eh? Kirsten saving Paul.'

'People surprise you,' I said, remembering the people in my short past who had amazed me. Gaby McGurk and Zoe, and Jake.

'I've texted my cousin,' Faisal said brightly.

'A secret item, a special delivery – if he's anything like you, Faisal, how can he resist it?'

'I can't get over what an exciting time we're having,

Noel,' Faisal went on. 'Though, you're not Noel, are you?'

'But you have to keep calling me that, Faisal. Keep up the pretence. I told you, the Dark Man's here somewhere. Thinks I might be the body they found on the moors.'

'I'll try. It won't be easy.' Faisal was nothing if not honest. 'I think of you as Ram already. The name must mean something. You can't just have chosen it at random. It must be the key to some dark secret. Maybe we can figure out what it is.'

The key to some dark secret, but what?

'No chance of your cousin's van coming today, I suppose?' I asked him.

Faisal shook his head. 'Only on a Friday.'

I would have to be patient. One more day. And I thought of the Dark Man. Had he found out the body on the moors wasn't me? Would that make him stay, or make him go?

I wished desperately I knew where he was.

32

The Dark Man was heading back to the Darlings. He would send this information and wait for instructions. He would probably be told to move on. He had to find that boy. If he began to remember all he knew the boy could ruin everything.

He turned the car from the road on to the school drive. Something was happening up ahead outside the school. He parked his car outside the house just as Mrs Darling came running out of the door. She looked angry. 'I've called the police! Why aren't they here yet? You have to help him.'

He stepped out of the car and looked down towards the schoolhouse. The teacher had a hold of a thin, wiry man. He recognised him: the stepfather, Wilkie. He had seen him earlier outside the police station. He had lost none of his anger. The man was thin, but used to fighting. The teacher wasn't. The teacher moved away from the man, turned his back on him, trying to avoid any trouble, but this Wilkie was having none of that. He grabbed Darling by the neck, pulled him back, kicked into his legs. The teacher stumbled, fell to the ground. Wilkie was almost on him then, but Darling managed to roll away from him, just in time. He got up on one knee, held out his hands to hold the man back. Must have seen he wouldn't stand a chance.

'He's not a fighter. You have to help him,' the woman pleaded.

Just then the teacher caught sight of him and began waving his arms about frantically, calling him over, wanting help.

It was the last thing he needed, but it would look too suspicious if he ignored this and did nothing. He had no choice.

&

Mr Darling had never been so glad to see anyone. He couldn't cope with Wilkie any longer. The man was crazy with anger. Powerful with it. When Wilkie saw the tall dark man heading for them that only made him angrier. He lashed out, caught the teacher's face and sent him reeling. Mr Darling fell back, saw McGuffin running towards them, saw him reach for Wilkie and in a second, he had him by the throat, hauling him back, his arm tight around his neck.

Wilkie, taken by surprise, arched his back. He was on tiptoe. His face turned bright red, then drained of any colour. For a moment, Mr Darling wanted to scream out, so sure McGuffin had broken Wilkie's neck. He looked powerful enough, and quick enough. And he thought . . . this is no businessman.

&

Faisal was watching at the window. He couldn't contain

his excitement. 'Mr Darling's mate, that Mr McGuffin's just turned up. He's got Wilkie in a stranglehold . . . like this . . .' He demonstrated on an imaginary victim. 'It's brilliant. Come and see.'

I was about to cross the room to look, but Kirsten came in. She looked really worried. 'You've got to come and talk to Paul. He knows he's out there. He's terrified.'

I called to Faisal as I ran after her. 'Keep watch, Faisal. Let us know if they look as if they're coming back in.'

Faisal didn't even turn round. He only waved his hand. I followed Kirsten.

Paul was shaking with terror, gone the bravado of earlier. I could see his body tremble with fear. No wonder. Faintly I could make out the shouts, the sound of the fighting. I was so glad this McGuffin had turned up to help the teacher. There was no way we could ever let the Wilkies of this world win.

'I hate him for making me feel like this.' Even Paul's voice trembled.

In the distance we could hear the police siren. 'He'll be gone soon,' I said. 'They'll take him away.'

'I hate them too.' And I knew he meant the police. 'Promise you won't tell them I'm here.'

'You don't even have to ask that,' Kirsten said. 'You know I'd never let that happen.'

A smile passed between them. Paul turned to me. 'I even trust you. It's Faisal that worries me. He tells his dad everything. He tells that family of his everything.'

I thought of Faisal's cousin. Maybe Paul was right – we should have left Faisal out of this. Too late now.

'We're getting you away, far away, tomorrow. I

promise.' Didn't add that I planned to be with him.

'But where is he going to go tonight?' Kirsten wanted to know.

I hadn't thought of that.

'Couldn't he stay in the shed?'

Kirsten looked at me as if I was stupid. 'Do you not think I'd have brought him here before if I could?' she snapped. 'Mr Darling checks everything and locks up after we leave. I'm not going to risk Paul being found.

'Why can't he go home with Faisal, then?'

That seemed to amuse both of them.

'Faisal has brothers and sisters, two aunties and a granny and his mum and dad all living with him. It's like the old woman who lived in a shoe in that house.'

I smiled too. 'Well, maybe they wouldn't notice one more.'

Paul almost managed a smile back. 'Wrong colour, I'm afraid.'

Way wrong, I thought. Paul's face was the colour and the texture of wax on a candle. I looked at Kirsten.

'Don't look at me. I brought him here for help. My dad's back tonight. I can't hide him any longer.'

'You're expecting me to help him?' I said. 'Have you forgotten? I'm living with a couple of homicidal maniacs. And you expect me to hide Paul?'

'You said you've been on the run, keeping out of the clutches of this Dark Man, making yourself out to be one of those urban heroes.'

'I'm not a hero,' I said.

'Whatever, you've been living by your wits. Surely for one night those wits can help hide Paul.'

She was right. I knew she was right the instant she said it. I didn't know how I was going to manage it, but Paul was coming home with me tonight.

✼

Faisal couldn't take his eyes off Mr McGuffin. He was full of admiration. The man was strong, a great fighter, the kind you could rely on in a crisis.

Not like poor Mr Darling. Faisal almost felt sorry for him. He was a bit of a wimp really. He tried – he was trying now – on his feet, pretending he was helping Mr McGuffin. But Mr McGuffin didn't need any help. He had Wilkie gripped so tight that it looked as if he tried to move he would break his neck.

Faisal tried to imagine his dad in a fight like that. The very idea made him smile. His dad would try to reason with him, make him see sense. Even if his dad was lying on the ground half conscious he still would be trying to reason with him.

But Mr McGuffin. Now, he was a different matter altogether. He was a man of action. No one would ever mess with Mr McGuffin.

The police car was coming. Faisal could hear its siren, see it racing off the road and on to the school drive. Wilkie was on the ground now, staying down. Mr Darling was standing over him. Mr McGuffin stepped back and after a word with the teacher he moved off back to the house. Faisal watched him go. He even walked like a hero – looked to Faisal like a hero wandering off into the sunset, or in this case . . . the fog.

He jumped when he realised a text was coming

through on his phone. He pulled it from his pocket and read the message.

So here was the next surprise. He almost called for Ram. No. He mustn't call him Ram. 'Noel! Kirsten!' he called through. They were in the classroom in seconds.

'My cousin's up for it,' he said, grinning. 'And he said something else as well.' Faisal hesitated, wanted to make the most of it. 'He says he's got a special delivery for us too.'

33

Moments later, the police came wailing into the yard. We all crowded round the window to watch as Wilkie was hauled into the car, shouting abuse, yelling vengeance, angry as ever. Mr Darling stood while a policeman took notes, glancing every now and then towards the schoolhouse.

'So where's this McGuffin guy?' I asked.

'Must have gone inside the house. Honest, you should have seen him. He was brilliant.' Faisal began dancing around, throwing punches, darting and diving like some demented boxer.

'Noel's offered to take Paul home with him tonight,' Kirsten said.

That made me laugh. 'Noel is being forced to take Paul home with him,' I reminded her.

Faisal looked surprised. I didn't blame him. 'How's he going to manage that?'

'*I* managed it,' Kirsten said. 'Kept him in the garage, brought him here in the boot of Mum's car.'

'That's what I'll do,' I said. 'You two will have to arrange some kind of diversion, get Uncle William away from the car so I can sneak Paul into the boot. OK?'

'That sounds simple.' Kirsten looked at Faisal. 'So simple even you might manage it.'

'I'm not as simple as you,' Faisal snapped back at her.

'That's it. That's what you do. You two quarrel, make sure Uncle William has to come into the classroom. I'll do the rest.'

Mr Darling was shaking. He hated confrontation – always had. This man was so full of hate, so full of anger and violence. He hoped Paul was far away from him, and stayed away, wherever he was. His wife had been right; he should never have allowed him to go back there. But it was too late now for guilt.

He had thanked McGuffin. How glad he was he came along when he did. He'd had Wilkie subdued in an instant.

Yet, that troubled him too. He didn't fight like a businessman. He had tackled Wilkie as if he had been trained to do it. Had he been a soldier once, he wondered? Was there something he wasn't telling them? He shook the thought away. He was looking for mysteries everywhere, like Faisal. It was this grey mist that hung over the hills. As if they were all locked into another world. It was claustrophobic. And it was the thought of a beast somewhere out there, roaming the moors, hungry, looking for prey.

And he thought again of the body on the moors. Who was it, if it wasn't Paul?

'What's the plan?' Paul asked. I had darted in to let him know that Wilkie had been taken away by the police. He looked more than relieved by that.

'OK, so you're coming back with me tonight,' I told him. 'You might have to sleep in the car, but I'll keep you safe.'

He just nodded his head, willing to do anything to keep out of the clutches of that evil man, Wilkie. I understood. Wouldn't I do anything to keep out of the clutches of the Dark Man? Had he heard the body wasn't Paul's? Would that make him stay in the area? Or had he already moved off? So many strangers were here anyway – reporters, media people – one more wouldn't look suspicious. Or was he following another clue he hoped might lead him to me?

Forget it, Mr Death, I thought to myself, *I beat you once. I can beat you again.*

'And tomorrow,' I went on, 'I'll bring you back here, same way, and you'll get away in Abdullah's van.' I hesitated. 'And I'm coming with you.' The thought of escape excited me. I was getting away at last from the madness that was Uncle William and Aunt Mary.

'I think I've figured out what the special delivery is,' Faisal said when I went back into the classroom, not a moment too soon. I could see Mr Darling striding back from his own house. He looked more sure of himself now. Faisal was right. He wasn't a fighter. But he was a good man, did his best to protect us.

'So, what is it?'

Faisal beamed. 'My birthday present. I heard my dad telling my aunties last week that Abdullah had a special surprise present for me. He said he was dying for me to see it. My cousin can't keep a secret.'

'And we're trusting him with Paul?!' Kirsten gasped.

Funny, how they had lapsed so easily into their old fighting relationship. In spite of the fact they had banded together to help a fugitive.

Faisal ignored her. 'I bet that's the special delivery. It will be the latest PlayStation game.'

Faisal grinned. It was hard not to smile back when Faisal smiled.

Mr Darling came into the class just then. 'Sorry about that,' he said. 'I'm afraid we had to call the police.'

'At least that's one less beast on the loose,' Kirsten said. A girl after my own heart.

'I won't press charges, Kirsten. Maybe the man's been through enough. He's been questioned because they thought the body was Paul's. And it wasn't. Until Paul is found he'll be under suspicion. Maybe that is punishment enough.'

And I knew then that though Mr Darling was a good man, a decent man, a man who would always try to do the right thing, Paul was right. He would always stay within the law. We'd been right not to tell him about Paul. Had we done that, Paul would be somewhere now, with well-meaning people, who would already be considering sending him back to Wilkie. No. It was up to me and Kirsten and Faisal to get Paul away, far away from here, safe.

34

'I just can't tell you how much I appreciate you helping, Mr McGuffin.' The woman, Mrs Darling, was so grateful it was embarrassing. He had headed for the house before the police arrived. Didn't want any involvement with them, and the teacher had assured him he wasn't going to press charges. He just wanted this Wilkie to be taken away, he had said, and to be kept away. 'I hate that man,' she went on, her voice bitter. She looked as if she had the cares of the world around her shoulders. 'I bet when you came to this quiet little outpost of civilisation you didn't think you'd end up in a fight.'

He shrugged.

'I'm so glad it wasn't Paul's body. Did you hear it wasn't Paul?'

'Yes, I heard that in the town.' He waited for her to go on.

'I hope he's far away from here. I hope they never catch him. Can you imagine living with that beast?' She waved her hands to where Wilkie had stood, threatening her husband, as if he was still there and she couldn't bear to look.

'They wouldn't send the boy back to him this time, surely?'

Her eyebrows shot up. 'Wouldn't they? We wanted to keep him, my husband and I, and they wouldn't let us. Can't break up a family, they said. A family! Ha! I would have hidden him here, that's what I would have done. But my husband . . .' There was a bitterness in the way she said it. A disagreement that always came between husband and wife. It wasn't hard to see that.

He decided to change the subject. The woman looked as if she was ready to cry.

'Any idea who the dead boy might be?'

'Maybe a hiker . . . though no one's been reported missing.'

'Do you get a lot of strange boys around here?'

'Everyone's a stranger passing through. The new boy, Noel Christie, he was supposed to start two weeks ago. Seems his family have had trouble with him too.'

'Yes, I met the uncle,' he said.

'Hope he's not another Paul. I couldn't bear it.'

'His uncle seemed really fond of him.'

'Yes, that's what my husband says. So why does he keep running away?' She sighed. 'Secrets, Mr McGuffin. Who knows what secrets are hidden behind closed doors.' She smiled. 'What's your secret?'

'Me?' he said. 'I'm an open book.'

Kirsten, I decided, was a brilliant little actress. She was standing beside me at Uncle William's car, stamping her feet, determined to be taken seriously. 'Mr Christie,

155

come and see what he's done!' It was a demand.

Uncle William hadn't expected that. He was ready to get back into the car and leave. He turned to her. 'Me?'

'Yes! I want a witness. Not his dad.' She poked Faisal in the chest, sent him staggering backwards. 'Not even my mum.' Kirsten's mum hadn't arrived yet. Always late to pick her up. Kirsten had been relying on that. She was already tugging at Uncle William's sleeve. 'Come on!' Kirsten never asked. She demanded.

Uncle William looked back at me. 'Get in the car, Noel.' That was the last thing I wanted to do. Once in the car, he'd set the locks, I'd be trapped in there. Kirsten knew that. So did Faisal. He pulled at Uncle William too. 'Come into the classroom. You'll see she did it herself. Then blames me.'

Kirsten started screeching. 'It *was* him!'

Uncle William had no choice. He looked back at me. 'Get in the car,' he said again. I did, but I left the door on the latch.

He was still worried I'd run. Why? Why did they want me so much? Want Noel? I had to find out.

I waited till he was safely inside the schoolhouse, out of sight, before I moved.

35

Mr Darling was trying to talk to Faisal's dad when Noel's uncle was dragged in very reluctantly by Kirsten. Faisal's dad was annoyed, and the teacher had never seen him annoyed before. He had brought his son up to respect people, even obnoxious people like Kirsten. And Faisal always had. He couldn't believe Faisal, his cheery happy son, had done anything so destructive. Neither could Mr Darling. But would Kirsten do it herself? And why? Attention seeking, the first answer that came to mind. Her father away, her mother always working. No attention ever really given to her.

All Mr Darling wanted was them all away, so he could close up the school, sit in comfort, just him and Millie . . . Then he remembered Mr McGuffin. Tonight they wouldn't be alone. And there was something troubling him about McGuffin. What was it?

He was dragged away from his thoughts by Kirsten's annoying whine. 'Mr Christie, look what he did!' She held up her jacket, ripped from sleeve to neck, slashed and torn. 'Who else could have done that?!'

'It wasn't me!' Faisal shouted again.

'Faisal, if you did this terrible thing, admit it!' Mr

Yusaf said.

Surely, Mr Darling thought, he didn't honestly think his son could do such a thing?

Mr Yusaf's eyes flicked to William Christie. 'I'm sorry to ask this, but could it have been your nephew? I know you've had problems with him.'

Before William Christie could answer Kirsten burst out. 'It wasn't Noel.' She still kept a grip on Noel's uncle. 'It was Faisal . . . I saw him do it!'

'That's a lie!' Faisal yelled at her. 'She did it herself, I bet, and now she's blaming me.'

'And why would I do that, stupid!' Kirsten yelled.

'Because you *are* stupid!' he yelled back.

Mr Darling saw William Christie's eyes flick to the door. Noel was in the car. He was scared his nephew would run away again. 'Look, I really have to go.'

'Of course you must,' the teacher said.

Kirsten was suddenly almost hysterical. She held on tight to his arm. 'Don't go, Mr Christie. They're all on his side. Please say you believe me!'

Paul was crouched at the door of the bike shed when I ran to get him. Not a second to waste. 'The boot's open. You jump in. I'll cover you with a blanket. Get you out at the cottage.'

My heart was leaping in my chest, but not for me. I was safe – Uncle William wouldn't do anything to me . . . not yet. My fear was for Paul if he was caught, and what would happen to him.

But he wouldn't be. I could wait one more day.

Tomorrow, Paul and I would leave together.

I held him back just before we made for the car. Checked towards the door of the schoolhouse to make sure we wouldn't be spotted. I could hear Kirsten's hysterical screaming, playing the spoilt little madam to the hilt.

'She's got a voice you could swing for, hasn't she?' Paul whispered with a grin.

'Come on.' I pulled him on and we ran. Our breaths burst in clouds in the cold foggy afternoon. I held open the boot. Paul scrambled inside. I laid the tartan blanket over him, hid him from view. 'When we get to the house I'll find a way to open the boot and let you out. OK?' I said.

'OK by me.'

'Good luck, Paul.'

'It's been with me so far.' He grinned again, fear gone for a moment, his teeth white against his grimy face.

I could still hear shouting from the classroom. Uncle William wouldn't be held there much longer. I snapped down the lid of the boot and jumped into the front seat.

They're holding me here deliberately, Uncle William was thinking. These two had their reasons. It was all an act. The stupid girl screaming. The boy yelling back at her. Both of them holding tight on to his sleeve. He was sure he knew why.

So the boy could run. He'd had enough of it. He jerked himself free of the girl with so much force she stumbled against the desk. The teacher looked startled.

Uncle William apologised. 'Look, I have to go. I've left Noel in the car. I can't risk . . .'

He didn't have to say any more. Even the stupid teacher understood.

'Let Mr Christie go. He has Noel to look after.'

The girl stood in front of him, blocking his way, stepping this way and that so he couldn't pass her. He wanted to throw her to the side. He knew now he was right. They were doing this deliberately. He was past her at last, out of the schoolhouse and into the yard, running to the car, sure it would be lying empty.

And he was there. Sitting in the front seat, just the way he'd left him.

And that puzzled Uncle William even more.

36

He heard the screaming and yelling as he lay in his room. Time to move on, the Dark Man was thinking. No point hanging about here. The body wasn't the boy's. The boy still lived.

What was all that noise outside? He tried to blot it out, to think. It was the girl's voice, demanding attention, screeching for it. He wished someone would shut her up.

It was no use. He couldn't ignore what was happening out there. He stood up, crossed to the window. From here he had a clear view of the schoolhouse. Dark would fall soon – already wisps of dusk had settled on the hills.

The man, Christie, was getting into his car. His face was grim with annoyance. Gone was the ever-present smile – annoyed by the noise the girl was making too, he supposed. He slammed the car door shut, looked at his nephew, puzzled about something. The Dark Man couldn't see the boy's expression, couldn't see his face at all in the passenger seat. Just that red jacket.

The car moved off. At the same time the girl stopped her whining. The Dark Man waited a moment, expecting it to start again. But she didn't. All was quiet at last.

He crossed back and flopped on the bed. If he could just find the boy. He was sure he was close. Why should he be so sure?

🏃

Uncle William didn't say a word all the way home. He glanced at me, watched me. Wondered. But I was still here. It might have puzzled him, but it was all that mattered. I said nothing either. My brain was in overdrive. I was trying to figure out how I would get Paul out of the boot without Uncle William spotting him.

He never let me leave the car till it was safely in the garage. Then he would walk with me to the cottage, making certain I wouldn't run off. Same every night.

We reached the cottage. He drove the car straight into the garage as usual, switched off the engine and turned to me. 'Ready, Noel?' he asked, still keeping up the pretence. Why? I couldn't understand. Here, at the cottage, they knew I wasn't Noel. That boy, the real Noel, I was convinced was the body that had been found on the moors.

But still they insisted on calling me Noel.

They were mad – the only explanation. I couldn't wait to get shot of these two.

Uncle William never locked the car. He walked to the door of the garage, and out into the misty night. I followed him. There was nowhere for me to go. He knew that. No other exit out of the garage.

At the door I called to him, 'Forgot my rucksack.'

'Hurry, then,' he said, but he waited by the cottage door, watching, making sure I came straight back out.

I raced back into the garage and opened the boot as quietly as I could. Paul was crouched inside. He peeked out from under the blanket. There was no fear in his eyes now. Only defiance. I liked that. He had survived this far. He was determined to keep on surviving. So was I. He leapt out of the boot without a word, dragging the blanket with him.

He slipped under a table in the far corner. 'Don't worry about me, I'll be fine here.' He smiled. 'I've been in worse places.'

'I'll try and bring food out later,' I said. Hadn't a clue how I would do it. I'd cross that bridge when it came.

He pulled the blanket over his head. Anyone coming in would never think there was anything, especially a human being, hiding under there.

I grabbed my rucksack. In a second I was hurrying back out into the darkening fog.

'Got it!' I held the rucksack high as I ran past Uncle William and through the open door of the cottage. Aunt Mary was waiting with one of her hearty meals.

I was glad now I had brought Paul back with me. We were going to be together from now on.

McGuffin had eaten his evening meal with them and gone back to his room. Mr Darling waited until he heard his footsteps in the room above before he said to his wife, 'Where did he learn to fight like that?'

'Perhaps he used to be a soldier,' she said.

That had been his conclusion too. 'I thought he was going to break Wilkie's neck at one point.'

Millie only shrugged. No sympathy for Wilkie at all.

He knew then she wouldn't talk about McGuffin. Maybe she thought he was more of a man than her husband. All he said was, 'I don't think he's any kind of businessman.'

Faisal had been grounded, which he considered to be completely unfair. He hadn't done anything. Although when he thought about it, being grounded wasn't such a punishment. He couldn't go outside anyway, because of the Beast. He wondered if they'd ever catch it. Maybe his dad was right and it was only a figment of someone's imagination. No one had actually seen it after all. But something had eaten the body on the moors. If it wasn't the Beast, what else could it be? He hoped it wasn't a puma after all. How boring was a puma?!

And what about Kirsten – hiding Paul all this time? If it wasn't completely against his better judgement he might even admire her.

And Noel not being Noel at all, but some mysterious runaway with no memory. It couldn't get any better than this, he thought.

Yet it had: watching Mr McGuffin fight like a hero. How he wished he could learn to fight like that. How he wished his dad could fight like that. He only ever talked himself out of trouble, or apologised. Like today, with Kirsten's mum. Apologising to her about something he'd never done.

He'd got into so much trouble because of that. The things he did for Paul. He hoped he appreciated it.

Paul. Was he safe with Ram? Maybe, Faisal thought, he should have taken Paul to his house instead.

Just then his Auntie Munan tiptoed into the room. 'My poor little Faisal. What kind of man is your father? A monster. A beast. A tyrant. A dictator!' Hardly sounded like his dad at all. 'Making you stay in your room. Here, I brought you some chocolate.'

A moment later his Auntie Furzana arrived. She brought him some Turkish delight. His favourite. 'Here you are, dear. I can't believe that father of yours has made you stay in your room.'

And any moment now his mother would come and then his granny. And Faisal knew this was the worst place Paul could be. Piccadilly Circus was quieter.

37

I sneaked food to the garage for Paul after dinner. Bread and cheese and thick slices of ham. Wrapped it in toilet paper and pushed it under the door the instant before Uncle William appeared in the beam of light from the cottage, checking on me, wondering where I was.

'Fresh air,' I said, and I breathed in. He didn't move till I'd come back inside the house, then he locked the front door and set the alarm.

Paul would think I had landed lucky when he saw that food, I thought. He'd wonder why I'd want away from here. If he'd heard what I had overheard earlier, he wouldn't wonder for long.

Aunt Mary and Uncle William whispering in the kitchen, thinking I was upstairs.

'Tomorrow's his last day at school,' Uncle William said. 'By the weekend it will be all over.'

And her tearful reply. 'I couldn't take much more of this, William. It has to be over by Monday.'

I didn't know what they were planning for this Noel over the weekend. And I wasn't hanging around to find out.

*   *   *

I awoke in the dark. There was no moon, and something was moving outside. There was a light dusting of snow on the window. I listened. What had woken me? I sat up in bed. My first thought was that I didn't want it to keep on snowing. That might mean they would keep me off school tomorrow. And Paul and I had to be there. I prayed for it to stop.

My second thought was . . . what was out there?

I crossed to the window. It was too dark. I could see nothing; even the snow brought no light. But there was something out there. I peered through the blackness, sure I could make out a movement, black on black. Was this the Beast, back looking for food? Down on the farmlands, searching for another sheep?

Was Paul aware of it too? What if it was at the garage right now? I imagined it pawing at the door, clawing it open, attracted by the smell of the food I'd brought earlier. And Paul, terrified, looking around for some-where to hide. I could almost see it happening. It would have the scent of Paul. And it had a taste for human flesh now.

All thought of escape deserted me in an instant. If the Beast was here, I would have to let everyone know Paul's hiding place. I would have to save him.

I gasped as I saw sleek black fur, no mistake. I stood back from the window, sure I could see the flick of a blue-black tail. But I was too afraid to look, could only imagine its green eyes waiting, watching. Watching me.

I don't know how long I waited in the darkness, listening, too terrified to move.

An age seemed to pass before I had the nerve to step closer to the window again and look.

There was nothing now. Black emptiness. But I was sure that the Beast had been there, and it had come for me.

38

FRIDAY

'Did you hear it last night?' I asked them. Uncle William was eating breakfast; Aunt Mary at the stove, cooking as usual. The smell of smoked bacon and sausages filled the kitchen.

'Heard what?' he asked, without even looking up.

They had to be joking! They hadn't heard the Beast, so close? But why would they lie about that? Another puzzle.

'It was here. Outside. I heard it. You must have heard it.'

'It wouldn't come near the houses, surely?' Aunt Mary put a plate dripping with food in front of me. I'd never be hungry again, I thought. She had given me enough food to keep me going for years to come.

Then I reminded myself, Aunt Mary didn't mean me to be here for years to come. So, why were they feeding me so well?

'Can I go out and see if there are any footprints?'

They glanced at each other. Afraid I'd run away again? But I supposed by now they realised there was nowhere for me to run away to.

'Well, eat up your breakfast first,' Aunt Mary said.

I gobbled it down, and grabbed a couple of chunks of bread and sausages to eat as I left. For Paul, of course. I'd slipped some bacon in my pockets too. Hoped he didn't mind the fluff. I knew they would be watching me at the window, see me study the ground, even see me step inside the garage. Why should they be suspicious of that? From the garage there was no escape either.

Kirsten heard her parents arguing again that morning. Her dad had come back and that was all they had done. Argue.

'You have to do something about it. Tell someone!' she could hear her father say.

And her mother had been in tears, angry tears. Her mother!

'You can't blame me. Not completely.'

Was their marriage breaking down? Were they talking about going to marriage guidance? Was her father about to leave for good?

She had thought it was because of this man. She had been sure of it. Now she didn't understand what was going on. Not after she had heard her mother crying. 'She's killed someone . . . and it's all my fault.'

Killed? What was going on? Was there another mystery here? Last night her dad had wanted to take Kirsten away from this place. He was going, he had said, and she could come with him. For her own safety, he had said. She had refused to go. That had upset him. Surprised him too. But she couldn't go away, not yet. Not today.

There was too much to do here.

'Well, I don't think you should go to school today at least.' Her father had made the suggestion and it had appalled her.

'No. I have to go. I don't want Faisal thinking I'm scared of him.'

Scared of him! Scared of Faisal? How could anyone believe that!

She couldn't possibly miss school today. Today they all had their job to do to help Paul to escape.

Kirsten was excited, just as she had been excited at the thought of hiding Paul. It still gave her a thrill. No one had known where he was, no one could find him. And he had been right under their noses all along.

She was meant for danger, she decided. Danger and excitement.

But who was the killer her mother was crying about, and why was it her fault?

Faisal's mother and his aunties and his granny all wanted him to stay off school today too.

'It's Friday,' his granny said. 'No boy learns anything on a Friday.'

'It looks like snow,' his Auntie Furzana said.

'That bad girl might cause him more trouble.' This was his Auntie Munan.

'I can't bear to think of my darling boy being stuck with that awful girl again.' His mother, of course.

Faisal was terrified his dad would bow to all this powerful female pressure.

As if.

His father had shaken his head. 'Faisal must face up to things. He will only look guilty if he stays off school.'

'I agree completely, Dad.' Now, that should have made his dad suspicious right away. Faisal was always looking for ways to stay off school, and he never agreed with anything his dad said.

But he had to go to school today. This was his big day. His stomach was in knots just thinking about it.

Hiding Paul in his cousin's van, making sure he got away safely – was this the way the people in the Resistance felt? His nerves taut like steel. His bowels ready to move at any moment.

And if they were caught . . . what would happen to them?

Worse, what would happen to Paul? A fate worse than death.

No. They had to succeed.

39

Paul was waiting for me, crouched under a workbench, still covered with the blanket. 'It's been freezing in here,' were his first words.

I was beginning to see what Kirsten meant. Paul always found something to complain about.

'Brought you some food,' I said. I took the bread and sausages and bacon and handed them to Paul. He took them with grimy fingers, began studying the bacon carefully, picking bits of fluff off it.

'Sorry,' I said.

I waited for him to moan about it, but he didn't. He shrugged. 'Suppose it's OK.' And he stuffed the crispy bacon into his mouth hungrily.

'You get fed well here,' he mumbled.

'Yeah, I don't know why. I still think they mean to kill me.'

Paul laughed. Breadcrumbs and bacon spluttered everywhere. 'Ever heard of Hansel and Gretel?'

Hansel and Gretel. I'd heard that before. Where? It rang a bell. I wanted to ask about them, but any moment now I was waiting for Uncle William to step into the garage and catch us. I had to get Paul back into the boot before that.

I held open the door for him. 'Did you hear it last night?' I was beginning to think it must have been my imagination.

But I didn't have to explain what I meant. Paul almost choked.

'Hear it? I was sure I was going to be its next meal. I shot back inside that boot again, ready to lock myself in, terrified.' His eyes flashed with fear at the memory of it. 'It was right outside. It scrabbled at the door. Clawed at it. It could have got in easy. I don't know why it didn't. It must have been able to smell the food you brought out. Smell me. They're supposed to be able to smell fear. And I was pissing myself.' He grinned again. 'Wonder why it didn't come inside?'

I was beginning to think I knew the answer. Jake's coat, the clothes I had arrived here wearing. They had all disappeared. Had they been left somewhere for the Beast to find? Was that why the Beast had come here last night? It wasn't interested in Paul.

It had the scent of someone else.

It had the scent of me.

The boy was still in the garage. What was he doing in there? He was becoming too suspicious. Mary was right. It was time it was over.

Today was Friday. His last day at school. With any luck, his last day.

He stepped inside the wooden garage silently, wanting to catch him . . . doing what? But there was the boy,

174

sitting in the front seat of the car. What was his game?

Uncle William got into the car beside him. The boy turned to him defiantly. 'I did hear it, you know,' he said.

Uncle William shrugged his shoulders, started the engine. 'Maybe you dreamt it. There's been so much happening, bound to be on your mind. Why would it come down here, sniff round a house like this?'

'Maybe it was hungry,' the boy said. He hadn't taken his eyes off Uncle William.

Uncle William drove the car carefully out of the garage. He waited till they were on the road before he answered him, looking at the boy and saying slyly, 'Maybe it was hungry for wicked little boys.'

He had hoped to scare him. But the eyes that stared back didn't look the least afraid.

And it was Uncle William who was scared.

40

It would snow again before long, I thought. The clouds hung heavy with the snow. The moors draped in a lacy shawl of snow. I said nothing on the journey, though I felt his eyes dart to me constantly. Let him wonder what was going on my devious mind. By tonight, I'd be gone. I was tense with the excitement of it. The daring of it. Me and Paul escaping together, right under their noses.

'Oh well, thank goodness it's Friday,' Uncle William said cheerfully. 'I am looking forward to the weekend.'

And I was able to turn and say quite honestly, 'So am I.'

'I'm so glad it's Friday,' Mr Darling said to his wife. 'I've hated this week. So much has happened. I'll be glad to put it behind me.'

'Let's move back to the city,' she said suddenly. 'It's quieter in the city.'

He was surprised she said that. She had hated the city since . . . He pushed the thought of it to the back of his mind. Now she actually wanted to go back? It was a good sign. She was getting better. He smiled at her. 'Yes, let's talk about that over the weekend.'

Maybe, he was thinking, Friday wouldn't be such a bad day after all.

Mr McGuffin sat at his laptop, sending a coded message. He'd leave today. Reluctantly. Some instinct still held him here. But the body on the moors was definitely not the boy he was looking for. There were no unidentified boys in this godforsaken place. There was nothing he should stay for now. And there was no time to risk the trail going cold. He'd wait for an answer to his message, and then he would move on.

I hadn't a clue how to handle the changeover this time. Uncle William wouldn't be so kind as to park right next to the bike shed so that Paul could sprint from the boot and hide inside. And it hardly seemed likely that Faisal and Kirsten could create a scene again. A bit too suspicious.

When we arrived, Faisal's dad was getting ready to drive away. Probably wanted off before Kirsten's mum arrived. He was too late. She drew up beside us and glared at him.

It was at that moment all hell broke loose.

Kirsten's mum stepped from her car. 'What on earth is that?' But she knew already what it was. 'The fire alarm!'

Suddenly, Faisal appeared at the door of the school. 'Dad! Dad! Help!'

I am sure Faisal's dad had never moved so fast. He was out of the car and racing for the school. Kirsten began to move too. Her mother held her back. She said sternly, 'You stay where you are. It might be dangerous in there.' She looked at Uncle William. 'Come on!'

Kirsten's mum hurried towards the school, expecting William to follow at her heels. He didn't have much choice, but there was no way he was going anywhere without me. He held on to my arm. 'Come on, Noel.'

I glanced at Kirsten. With just a lift of one eyebrow – you would have missed it in an instant – I knew she was ready to handle everything. It was as if I had been reading her eyebrows for years. Kirsten would get Paul out of the boot and into the bike shed. I could leave it all to Kirsten.

I pulled free of Uncle William's arm. 'Do you really think it's a fire?' Sounded just like any other boy eager for a drama. He almost tripped in his hurry to catch up with me as I ran towards the school, afraid I was about to sprint to freedom.

Faisal was standing, shamefaced, when we went into the classroom. 'It was an accident, Dad,' he was saying. 'It could have happened to anybody.'

Kirsten stepped in a moment later. 'Ha! It could have happened to any other idiot, you mean.'

Her mother turned on her angrily. 'Kirsten, don't you dare speak to anyone like that!'

Faisal jumped in the air. 'See! That's the way she talks to me all the time. I'm the one who's being bullied.'

'Oh, shut up, you wimp!'

They were shouting at each other. It was Mr Darling

who bellowed, 'By the end of this day, you two are going to be friends. And over the weekend you will both write a five-hundred-word essay on "How to treat people with respect".'

Kirsten giggled. 'Him! Write five hundred words? He doesn't know how to string five words together, let alone five hundred.'

I tried not to smile. They were holding them here, making sure Paul had enough time to hide himself in the bike shed.

They were a good team. Faisal and Kirsten.

41

'Why don't you leave after lunch?' Mrs Darling suggested. 'The snow should hold off till then.'

Her husband thought there was something strange about Mr McGuffin, something he didn't trust. But she would be glad of the company. She had realised she liked having someone to talk to. 'Abdullah's van's due soon. I'll get some lemon sole. You're not a vegetarian, are you?'

'Oh no,' he said. 'I eat anything.'

She waited for his answer. She hoped she didn't seem too eager. He smiled a dark smile. 'I will stay. I'm waiting for an important message anyway.'

'Can I show Noel some of my work on the computer, sir?'

Mr Darling was busy with Faisal. He looked up. 'Good idea, Kirsten.'

We sat at the only computer in the class, already switched on, waiting.

Kirsten nudged me and whispered, 'Have you thought of clicking on to the Missing Persons site?

Maybe someone's looking for you?'

The thought excited me. 'Is there a site like that?'

'Of course there is.' She glanced at the teacher to make sure he wasn't looking. 'You can find anything on the internet.'

If that was true then I must be able to find out something about myself, find out who I was. Find out if someone was looking for me. And someone had to be. A boy my age doesn't just go missing and no one searches for him. Paul was unloved, and half the police force in the country were out looking for him. Surely someone must be looking for me?

Kirsten brought her own documents up on the screen, before she clicked on the internet search button.

'So how are we going to get Paul into this van?' I asked softly as we waited for a connection.

'Easy,' Kirsten said. 'Faisal and I have it all worked out. Abdullah always takes groceries into the house and Mrs Darling always gives him tea, sometimes even lunch. Mr Darling gives us a break and joins them in the house. He's always in there for ages on a Friday. That's when we get the chance to sneak Paul into the back, hide him behind the boxes and things.'

'When did you sort all this out?' I asked.

'Last night, on our mobiles.'

'Even the fire-alarm trick?'

Kirsten grinned. 'Good, wasn't it?'

'You are good actors. You really would think you didn't like each other.'

'That's not acting!' she said. 'I can't stand Faisal.' She grinned at me, and the real Kirsten shone through. The girl who loved danger.

'It's so exciting, isn't it? Don't you just love it?'

I smiled back at her. 'Kirsten, I have no memory. But I've already been involved in a murder, and now I'm living with a couple of nutcases. Excitement . . . I don't need.' I glanced at the teacher now, then bent closer to Kirsten and whispered, 'I'm going with Paul.'

She didn't say anything. But I could see her working out all the implications of this in her head. Would Paul still be safe? Would this be a risk to him? She'd looked after Paul all this time. She felt responsible; didn't want anything going wrong now.

'I won't let anything happen to Paul. I promise.'

She smiled. 'Well, you've been looking after yourself OK, I suppose. He'll be in safe hands.'

I didn't want to remind her then of the Dark Man, and the danger I was already in. Wrong time. And anyway, just then the screen flashed and long lists of websites lay before us. All of them about Missing Persons. Had so many people gone missing? So many young people among them. So many people looking for them. Photographs of beloved children and pleas from distraught parents.

Come back. I love you.

All is forgiven.

We can work everything out. Just come home.

We moved from one site to another. More and more children. Why had they all run away? Safer on the run than at home . . . like Paul? It depressed me. Scared me.

But what scared me most of all was that there was no mention of me in any of those sites. No boy of my age or description that people were anxiously searching for.

'Why is nobody looking for me, Kirsten? Does nobody care about me at all?' The thought hurt more than I could bear. 'Who am I, Kirsten? Who exactly am I?'

42

We were all jumpy, waiting anxiously for the white van to weave its way up the winding track to the school. A light snow had begun to fall and Mr Darling announced that if it kept up we'd all be sent home early. Had he expected us to be delighted? I could see by the lift of his eyebrows he was surprised by our reaction to that.

'I couldn't go home early,' Kirsten said. 'There's no one at my house.'

'You can come home with me,' Faisal said cheerily. 'There's always someone at my house.'

'No, thank you!' Kirsten said. 'I'd rather chew glass.'

Mr Darling calmed them both down. 'Enough!' He glanced at me. What was he thinking? I puzzled him as much as I puzzled Uncle William – but not enough to do anything about it. He wouldn't have to puzzle much longer anyway. By the time the others were being sent home, I'd be long gone. Me and Paul. I was straining at the leash to get away.

'Maybe if we get sent home after lunch, Ram could come home with me.'

Mr Darling turned on Faisal. 'Ram? Who's Ram?'

Faisal's cheek flushed. He hit his head dramatically.

'Duh! What am I like? I mean Noel.'

'Dunderhead!' Kirsten snapped at him. 'Honestly, when they were handing out brains you must have been at the back of the queue . . . or in the wrong queue, probably.'

'And you must have missed out on the personality handout.'

She was starting an argument to cover Faisal's blunder.

The clock seemed to inch its way forward towards noon. I couldn't keep my eyes from the road, desperate for Abdullah's van to appear.

Faisal was desperate too. Why was his cousin always late when he was waiting for him? He checked his watch for the umpteenth time. Maybe there had been an accident. He imagined the van overturned on the lonely road. Food, cans, fish, meat, and his cousin sprawled all over the tarmac.

Just Faisal's luck for that to happen today!

Or maybe . . . he had been caught by the Beast! He pictured it leaping from a rock (though what exactly this creature looked like he couldn't say . . . but he could imagine: fangs, horns, claws, a monster breathing fire from its nostrils – his imagination went crazy when he thought about it). He saw it landing on the top of the van, tearing open the roof with its massive claws, driven to distraction by the smell of chops and Mars bars and cornflakes. He could picture Abdullah driving like a madman, swerving this way and that, trying to throw it from the roof until finally, just as the Beast is about to sink its fangs into his neck, he leaps from the front seat, and the van and the Beast roar over the cliff road, hurtle down into the chasm, burst into flames . . .

Hey, wait a minute! He reminded himself that his cousin was bringing him his birthday present. A special delivery. The last thing Faisal wanted was for it to go hurtling down a cliff.

At last, he heard the familiar clunk of the engine.

'It's the van! It's the van!' he shouted.

Kirsten tutted. Looked bored. 'Doesn't take much to please you, does it, pea brain?'

Mr Darling had to laugh. 'Faisal, you'd think you hadn't seen your cousin in years.'

But it had come at last. Faisal jumped to the window, watched its progress down the uneven track to the school.

Now was the time to spring into action.

Mrs Darling always looked forward to young Abdullah coming on a Friday. Fresh fish, fresh crusty loaves, and especially his chat. He would come in for tea and her husband would join them, sometimes he would even stay to lunch.

She could hear Mr McGuffin moving about upstairs. Should she ask him if he'd like to come down for coffee? He seemed to prefer his own company. In fact, he seemed preoccupied, his mind somewhere else entirely. Yet, it was his coming that made her realise how much she missed company.

He'd said he'd have lunch with them. Maybe he didn't want to be bothered before that, waiting for that important message. *But it can't do any harm just to ask him*, she thought. *After all, he doesn't have to come if he doesn't want to.*

Mr Darling had never seen Faisal so excited by the arrival of his cousin's van. Kirsten supplied the answer.

'He thinks his cousin's brought him his birthday present.' She seemed annoyed. 'Him and his PlayStation games. Do boys never grow up?!' Why was Kirsten always so annoyed by Faisal?

What had it all been about yesterday? Faisal bullying Kirsten. It had all been nonsense. Faisal was an open book. It was Kirsten who was deep, hiding secrets. He had felt that about her for, how long? For as long as the Beast had been loose on the moors. Since Noel had arrived. Was there a link here?

Or was it something else entirely?

'Are you going to ask him to park the van as close to the door as possible so we can get in the back of the van, sir?'

'Of course I will. But please, be extra careful, won't you?'

Faisal went outside with Mr Darling to talk to his cousin, while Kirsten and I waited impatiently in the classroom.

'We can bring Paul through the classroom,' she said,

'and get him right into the back of the van. Help him to hide himself in there. No one will be able to see from the house.' Then she turned to me with a frown. 'You better not spoil this for Paul.'

'I won't. You said the van leaves way before Mr Darling comes back from lunch. I'll be long gone before then, and I'll have Paul and me out of the van and safe somewhere before they figure out how we got away.'

She didn't want Paul caught now, and neither did I. Because if he was caught, I would be too.

'You must see I've got to do it, Kirsten. I can't stay here. Whatever they're planning to do, they're not planning for me to come back to this school on Monday.'

'I know. I understand. You have to find out what this secret is you have locked in your memory. You have to stay out of the clutches of the Dark Man. You told us. But . . . I just couldn't bear it if Paul was caught.'

'I told you. I'll look after him.'

Faisal bounced in. 'Get Paul. Quick! My cousin's gone up to the house.' His eyes lit up. 'He says my surprise is in the back of the van. 'Come on. I'm dying to see what it is.'

I hurried through the back door of the class into the old bike shed. Paul was standing ready. He'd heard the van coming too. He looked as excited as Faisal. 'I can't believe I'm going,' he said.

'We both are,' I said. 'Remember? I'm coming with you.'

He grinned, his teeth starkly white in his still unwashed face. I think he was glad of the company.

I led him from the classroom. Kirsten was keeping

watch for anyone suddenly appearing from the house. She turned when she saw Paul. I'd have sworn there were tears in those eyes if it had been anyone else but Kirsten.

They stood looking at each other.

'I'll never be able to thank you,' Paul said. 'I'd be back with him if it wasn't for you. Or I'd be dead, up there on the moors.'

Kirsten only shrugged as if it was nothing. 'Just don't get caught now.'

'I'll be careful, I promise.' I was almost waiting for them to hug each other. I'm sure that's what they wanted to do. But they didn't. Paul reached out and squeezed Kirsten's hand, and she touched his hand and smiled. Then Faisal was there, hurrying us on.

'Come on! No time to waste.'

No time to waste. We were out in the cold air. Faisal pulled the back door open and three steps came down automatically. He was as keen to see his present as he was to save Paul. In the back of the van boxes were stored and stacked high to the roof – a truly great place to hide. Right at the back, behind the boxes, unseen by anyone – able to sneak out when the van stopped and Abdullah opened the doors for us at another place. I could see Paul and I leaping, escaping out into some distant town, melting into the shadows. I'd be safe from Uncle William and Aunt Mary then, safe from the Dark Man too. And I wouldn't be alone any more.

'I wonder where my present is,' Faisal said, moving boxes and packets aside.

'Stuff your present.' Kirsten still stood outside the

van, keeping watch. 'Get Paul hidden.'

There was a shuffling sound just then at the back of the van. We all heard it.

'Are there mice in here?' Paul asked.

'Must be a pretty big mouse,' I said, as the boxes at the back began to shift and something emerged from the shadows.

But it wasn't a mouse.

It was a boy.

Faisal stumbled back, almost fell. Kirsten took a step inside the van.

They were shocked. But not half as shocked as I was.

Because I'd seen this boy before.

In an old photograph.

The boy was Noel Christie.

43

It was as if time had stood still. 'You're Noel Christie,' I said.

His face was thinner, paler, but unmistakeable. The face in the photograph. Noel Christie. But what was he doing here?

Kirsten took a step closer. 'What do you mean . . . he's Noel Christie?'

Faisal looked stunned. 'That's what I was going to say. He's Noel Christie too?!' His eyes flashed from me to the real Noel Christie, then he shook his head. 'I'm totally mixed up.'

'You're called Noel as well?' The real Noel Christie's face seemed to drain to grey.

I nodded. 'Noel Christie, live with Uncle William and Aunt Mary . . .'

He staggered back, as if I'd hit him in the chest. 'Uncle William and Aunt Mary.' He said their names as if they were a nightmare. 'I don't understand. You're with them?'

I didn't understand either. Why was he here? Couldn't be a coincidence. Didn't believe in coincidences.

Paul was beginning to get agitated. We'd forgotten

about him. 'Please, explanations later on.' He pulled at Kirsten. 'Help me with these boxes.'

Kirsten jumped. 'Get in the corner, Paul,' she ordered. Then she looked at me. 'We've not got time to waste.'

Millie was reluctant to let Abdullah go. She was disappointed he couldn't stay for lunch. Mr Darling knew how much she enjoyed his company on a Friday. He was a lot like Faisal. Full of chat, full of enthusiasm. She needed that. Hadn't she even enjoyed the company of McGuffin?

He could hear his footsteps pacing overhead. He hadn't joined them. Waiting for an important message, he'd said. There was something about him that Mr Darling didn't trust. He wished he could put his finger on what it was.

He realised Abdullah was talking to him. 'You're in dreamland, Mr Darling,'

'I'm sorry. So much has been happening this week.'

'I know, I've been hearing. I was so glad the body wasn't Paul's. At least there's still a chance that he's alive.' He said it as if he really didn't believe that could be possible. Neither did Mr Darling. He would always hear that threat in his nightmares. 'I'll snap him in two.' The violence, the anger of Wilkie. He should never have allowed Paul to be sent back there. Now it was too late. No matter how much Wilkie protested his innocence, Mr Darling was sure Paul was dead, and Wilkie had killed him.

'You're sure I won't be found here?' Paul slipped into the space behind the boxes.

'Yes.' Faisal was sure. 'I've been with my cousin lots of times when he's done his rounds. Look, you can trust him. Even if he moves the boxes he'll make sure you're still hidden in there.'

'Come on,' Paul urged me. He even moved aside to give me space.

Faisal looked at me. 'You're going too?'

I nodded.

Faisal grinned. 'I thought you might. Good,' he said, and then he glanced at the door of the house for any sign of someone coming out. 'Better get in, then.'

This was it. I would never know why the real Noel was here. Another mystery in my life. It seemed to be full of them. What difference would one more make?

'What are you going to do?' I asked him.

Noel smiled, and for a moment I saw the resemblance to his uncle. 'Revenge,' he said. 'I want revenge.'

I wanted to ask him more, but Faisal was becoming more agitated. 'Abdullah will be back any time. He wants to be well away before Mr Darling finishes his lunch. Come on.'

Kirsten dragged Noel out of the van. She glanced back once at me. 'Good luck,' she said. Then they were gone. Faisal began to push me. 'You're escaping, Ram. Maybe you're going to save the world with that secret of yours. Maybe it's something as big as Operation

Overlord. And I've helped.'

Yeah. I was escaping. I was getting out of this place at last.

44

Abdullah looked at his watch. 'I should be going, I suppose. That cousin of mine should have found his surprise by now.' He grinned. 'Children and their secrets, eh?'

Mr Darling tried not to smile. Abdullah was just seventeen, hardly more than a child himself. He finished his tea. 'I always enjoy my time with you, Mrs Darling.' Then he turned to the teacher. 'Now, don't you be thinking I'm trying to run off with your lovely wife.'

Mr Darling stood up when he did. 'I should be getting back and checking on them before lunch.' He was sure the pupils, Faisal especially, had something planned. He hoped he wasn't playing another of his tricks on Abdullah. Mr Darling still winced at the memory of the time he'd let off a stink bomb in the back of the van.

'They'll be fine,' Millie said. 'Abdullah will make sure they're back in the schoolhouse, won't you, Abdullah?'

Abdullah was reluctant to leave the warmth and the company. 'Of course I will. You stay here, Mr Darling, have a relaxing lunch. The pupils will be safe from this creature. I've seen no sign of it as I drive over the moors. Perhaps it doesn't exist at all.'

'But the body on the moors. It was . . .' His wife couldn't say it. It had been a child's body after all. Mauled and half eaten, not a memory to linger over.

'That could have been a wolf,' Abdullah said with decision. 'I think this creature is just a publicity stunt. To bring tourists round here.'

'You mean, like the Loch Ness Monster?' Mr Darling suggested.

That idea appealed to Abdullah. 'Yes, exactly. Look at the cottage industry that has built up around the Loch Ness Monster.'

Mr Darling could see young Abdullah's business brain trying to work out how he could cash in on the legend of the Beast.

'No one's been eaten by the Loch Ness Monster,' Mrs Darling said flatly.

'Yes, there is that, I suppose,' Abdullah said. He took Mrs Darling's hand and shook it. 'I will see you next week. If you want anything special, give me a call and I'll bring it for you.'

He turned to Mr Darling now. 'You look so glum. But by next week, the fog will have lifted, the weather will be clearer and so will your mind.'

'Always the optimist, Abdullah.' But he was, and Abdullah always lifted both his and Millie's spirits too. He hoped Abdullah was right. And that by next week, things would be different.

I slid down behind the boxes with Paul. I was trembling. By tonight I would be . . . where would I be? I didn't know. But I would be far away from the Dark Man and Uncle William and Aunt Mary. Wasn't that what I wanted more than anything?

This was self preservation. The most vital thing, wasn't it? I had to save myself. I had something in my memory, locked in there; something so important the Dark Man wouldn't give up till he caught me, found out what I knew, killed me.

'You OK?' Paul whispered. 'You're talking to yourself.'

I squeezed down beside him. 'Yeah,' I said absently. 'Do it all the time.'

But I was thinking. The real Noel had arrived. Why was he here? What had brought him here? What were Aunt Mary and Uncle William planning?

It didn't matter, I kept telling myself. I could live without knowing, without ever finding out. I might not live if I stayed here.

I saw Faisal smile, move away from the back doors of the van. His cousin was coming back and he was going forward to greet him, closing the back doors on us to keep us hidden. Soon the van would move off and take us both away to safety.

Seconds to decide.

'I can't go.' I turned to Paul.

'What?' He looked amazed. 'What do you mean? What are you staying for? We could get away from here.'

'I know. I'm stupid. But I can't. I have to find out Noel's story. What Aunt Mary and Uncle William are up to.'

'Maybe they're up to killing you,' he said.

'I know. But why?' Curiosity, that's what was driving me. I had to find out. Couldn't leave and never know. 'I'll survive,' I told Paul. 'It'll take more than Uncle William and Aunt Mary to kill me.'

I had to go. I edged out from behind the boxes, careful not to knock them over. 'You'll survive too, Paul. Now you're free, don't let them get you.'

Paul's eyes seemed to glow in the dark of the van. 'Don't intend to. Maybe we'll meet again.'

I stepped back. 'Good luck, Paul.'

Then, swiftly and silently, I slipped out of the van. Even if anyone saw me jump from the back, what had I been doing wrong? Nothing. Taking my time to choose a treat. I hurried back into the classroom. A moment later, Abdullah got into the van. Faisal stood waving at him, and I watched from the door of the schoolhouse as the van bumped up the rough track and turned on to the road. My chance of escape, my chance of freedom, and I had let it go.

45

The snow had begun to fall. Mr Darling looked out of the window. 'I think I will send them home early. I'll phone round, get them picked up.'

Millie came in from the kitchen. 'Will Kirsten's mother be there? She seems never to be at home.'

'Her father should be there.' He sighed. 'Kirsten can be so deep. You never know what she's thinking. And all that carry on with Faisal. What was that about? And Noel too. I wish I knew what was going on there.'

'Something's going on?' McGuffin had just come into the kitchen. He smiled at Millie. 'Hope I'm not intruding.'

'Not at all,' she smiled back. 'Lunch is ready. I was just about to call you.'

Mr McGuffin sat down.

'I'm just talking about my pupils. They all seem to have secrets.'

'And what kind of secrets would a child have?' his wife asked.

Mr McGuffin looked at her. 'You'd be surprised the secrets young people have.'

He said it as if he knew their secrets. His voice was

cold. A shiver ran down Mr Darling's spine, and he couldn't explain why.

Kirsten and Faisal looked astonished when I ran into the classroom.

'You didn't go?' Kirsten asked.

'Couldn't. Had to find out why he's here.'

Noel, the real Noel Christie, was sitting near the door to the bike shed, ready to run, to hide if Mr Darling should suddenly make his way from the house.

'I'm famished,' was all he said. 'Anything to eat?'

'Just like Paul – always after food.' Kirsten rolled her eyes.

I threw him my sandwiches. They'd been meant for him anyway. 'Your Aunt Mary made them,' I said.

'Sure they're not poisoned?'

I sat beside him. 'They've been treating me very well, pretending I'm you.'

He looked puzzled. 'And you let them?'

Faisal, keeping watch at the window, turned for a moment. 'He's lost his memory. Doesn't know who he is. But someone's after him, and we think he has a terrible secret locked in his memory, and they're going to kill him before he remembers it.'

'Thought for a while I *was* you,' I said. 'They were so convincing. Till I saw the photo.'

'You saw a photo?'

'A wedding or something. Uncle William was there. And you . . .'

'The photo's in the house?' Noel was eating the sandwiches hungrily.

I nodded. 'I put it inside one of the books on the bed-side table.' I watched him as he ate. He was my height, even had my colouring – dark hair just like mine, flick-ing over his brow. No wonder they wanted me to be Noel. We did look like each other.

'So why are you here? Can't be coincidence.'

'It isn't,' he said. 'I knew exactly where they'd moved to. I've been making my way here from London. Yesterday I was asking how to get a bus here, and some-one told me about Abdullah and how he did his rounds on a Friday, so I hitched a lift. I'm here to get them, to pay them back. I'm here for revenge.'

'Revenge? Why, what did they do to you?'

Noel smiled. I wished that smile didn't remind me so much of Uncle William. It made me shiver. But it was his next words that made me shake.

'They murdered me.'

46

'So, it's going to be tonight?' Aunt Mary sounded excited.

Uncle William looked at her fondly. He really had found his perfect partner in Mary. 'I haven't seen you this happy for so long.'

'I know, but I've been so worried about it since it happened. I'm trying not to think about that. It caused us all these problems. He just wasn't supposed to die then. It really wasn't my fault, was it, William?'

Uncle William assured her it wasn't. 'That boy was always a trial to us.'

'Well, he's gone now. Dead and gone.'

'And by tomorrow, forgotten.'

Faisal forgot about keeping watch. He darted to a seat beside Noel. 'Murdered? You're a ghost! You're not really here. Is that what you're trying to say?'

He grabbed at Noel's arm, pinched it. Noel yelped and pulled away from him. 'Do you mind? I'm real. Solid, flesh and blood. Hate to disappoint you, but I'm not a ghost . . . but they think I am.'

Kirsten had taken Faisal's place by the window. 'Explain what you mean. They murdered you?'

'My parents died a few months ago,' Noel said.

'Car crash,' I said. 'They told me.'

'Did they tell you I was left a very rich boy? A trust fund had been set up for me.'

'And if you die it all goes to Uncle William and Aunt Mary.'

Noel nodded.

'All this is about money?' Kirsten asked.

'Oldest motive in the world,' Noel said.

'So they think you're dead. The money's theirs,' Faisal said. 'Why pretend Ram is you?'

'Because it had to look like an accident. If anything happened to me they'd be the prime suspects, remember. I knew they were planning to kill me. I heard them talk about it. Heard them talk about moving here. It was just when the rumours of a creature on the moors were first in the news. This place is so remote; there was a small school with only a few pupils. A school that was getting ready to close. What could be better than a genuine terrible accident to a boy who kept running away? Perfect plan. The Beast gets me. They get the money.'

'Why didn't you tell someone?' Faisal wanted to know.

'I tried. Who'd listen? Uncle William and Aunt Mary are so caring, everyone would say. Taking me in after my parents died. Telling everyone how worried they were about me because I couldn't come to terms with my parents dying. That's why I kept running away, why I kept telling lies. Oh, they had it all sussed. Anyway, I'd lived with my parents in Australia. I hardly knew anyone here.'

'So no one to identify you here, but Uncle William and Aunt Mary?' I was beginning to understand. 'Only you spoiled their perfect plan by getting murdered too soon?'

He began to laugh as if the memory was funny. 'Aunt Mary did it. She didn't even mean to. I was trying to get away, yelling at her that I knew what they were planning to do and I wasn't going along with it. I'd get them. Told her I knew they'd caused the crash that killed my mum and dad too.'

'They did that?'

Noel's face went pale. 'It was just a guess, but I knew it was the truth as soon as I saw her face. They killed my parents.' He looked round us. 'Do you wonder why I hate them?'

'So what happened next?' I asked him.

'We were at the top of the stairs and she was so angry when I said that. So surprised, that she pushed me. All I can remember was her face, pure white with shock, trying to haul me back, realising it was too late. She couldn't stop me falling. I thought, *I'm going to die*. Have you ever felt like that?'

I shivered all over. Yes, I had felt like that. I remembered being trapped in the boot of a car, sinking underwater. Sure I was about to die. Preparing myself for death.

Another memory whipped through me, zooming through my subconscious like a rocket. Yes, I had felt like that another time too. Knew I was about to die . . .

in a dark place. Yet I wanted to stay, didn't want to run. Something, someone had saved me . . . Who? When . . . ? The memory snaked out of my head in a second, as quickly as it had come.

'They thought I was dead,' Noel went on. 'Thought they'd killed me, and how could they possibly make this look like a genuine accident? There would be an investigation and they would be the prime suspects.'

We were all asking questions at once. 'You said they thought you were dead?'

'Did they just leave you there?'

'What did they do with your body?'

'They must have panicked,' Noel said, biting into the bread hungrily. 'I wasn't supposed to die then, remember? They couldn't have anyone find me. So they put me in the chest freezer in the cellar. Can you imagine?' He seemed amused by the idea of it. I was horrified.

'But how did you survive?' I tried to imagine being trapped in there, like being locked in a coffin of ice.

'I think it was the freezer that probably saved my life. Slowed my metabolism or something. It was a bit of luck that a couple of neds, just young guys, saw Aunt Mary and Uncle William leaving the house, car packed up as if they were going away for good, and took a chance to break in, see what they could get.' He stifled a laugh. 'You should have seen their faces when they opened the freezer and I sat up.' He mimicked their panic. I only saw terror and fear. 'I have never seen anyone running so fast in my life. I will never say a bad word about hoodies again.'

'If Aunt Mary and Uncle William find you, Noel . . .

they might just finish the job.' I was genuinely worried about him.

Noel shook his head. 'But don't you understand? They think I'm dead. When you believe someone's dead you don't try to find them, do you?'

He was right. And maybe that was why no one was trying to find me. Everyone thought I was dead. Why?

'And I was the perfect replacement. The boy with no past, no identification,' I said. 'They needed me to take to this school where no one had met the real Noel, to be identified as the one and only Noel. The boy who keeps running away. So when my body is found, they can identify it as Noel, their nephew, the boy Mr Darling says is Noel, the boy Faisal and Kirsten say is Noel.'

'No one really knows me here. Who would doubt them? Who would blame them?'

Faisal said to me, 'Bit of luck you coming along when you did.'

But I had already thought about that. 'Maybe I wasn't the first. The body on the moors. A boy our age. It's not Paul, and it's not Noel. Maybe they'd found another boy, but he ran off before they had a chance to establish him as Noel.'

'Maybe they killed him too,' Noel said softly.

Kirsten gasped. 'How evil can these people be?'

I thought again of the Nazis and knew there were still evil people in the world. I thought of the Dark Man.

47

'We have to tell Mr Darling! He's our teacher,' Faisal said. 'He'll know what to do.'

Noel agreed. 'Yes, we'll go to him together.' He looked at me. 'You and I, the real Noel and the one they've been trying to pass off as their nephew. Prove the kind of people they are.'

'No.' I was having none of that. 'I can't. Any publicity and the Dark Man could find me. And what do I tell the police? I don't even know who I am. I don't know who to trust. No. That's out.'

Noel stopped. He shrugged his shoulders. 'OK, fair enough . . . Let's go back to plan A.' Noel was obviously a quick thinker.

'Plan A?' Faisal asked. 'What's that?'

'Well, I came here in the first place to give them the fright of their lives, didn't I? Get my revenge on them. Hey, hey, you thought I was dead, dear Aunt Mary and Uncle William, and then I walk in, larger than life!'

That really appealed to Faisal. 'Brilliant!'

Kirsten was staring at me. 'What's wrong with you?'

But my mind was thinking up an even more daring plan than the Resistance. If it worked out, it would be revenge all round. And I could melt into the shadows once more.

I explained to them then exactly what I had in mind. '. . . And we could call it Operation Noel.'

'Operation Noel. I love it!' Faisal said.

Kirsten was suddenly laughing. 'I'm up for that!'

Noel turned to me. 'This means I have to come back with you. You have to hide me.'

'You need to realise, Noel,' I said, 'that is the daftest thing you could do. I was running because they have something planned for this weekend – my untimely death, if you ask me. Or yours.'

'You don't understand. I'm already dead. Why should I be scared of them?'

Kirsten said, 'He's right, Ram. They think he's dead. And if your plan is going to work, he has to be there.'

I knew that, but I realised too that Noel could go to the police right now, and they would have to believe he was the real Noel. 'You're doing this for me,' I said.

'Don't you believe it. I love the sound of Operation Noel. Best revenge I could get. I'm doing this for me,' he said.

'Anyway, you have to get away,' Kirsten said to me. 'I still think you should have gone with Paul.'

I knew that was true. By now I could be somewhere far away, with a companion. Away from the Dark Man. But I wasn't. No time for regrets. If Operation Noel worked out, I would be out of here tonight, up and over the moors, on the run again. Nothing would stop me.

The snow was beginning to fall, tiny flakes landing on the ground, melting into nothing.

'I think we'll be sent home soon,' I said.

'And then Operation Noel, we have lift off!' Faisal said cheerfully. 'We've got our part to play, Kirsten. Me Batman, you Robin!'

'More like Hansel and Gretel.' Kirsten sniffed.

Hansel and Gretel, there it was again. 'Who are these two, Hansel and Gretel?' I asked.

'*Hansel and Gretel* – it's a fairy story,' Kirsten explained, 'about a brother and sister who are kidnapped by a witch. She traps Hansel in a cage, and feeds him so well he just gets fatter and fatter, because she wants to eat him.'

I couldn't believe it. 'That's a children's story? That's disgusting!' But something else shocked me more. 'Hansel and Gretel! That's what Aunt Mary has been doing to me. She's been feeding me up. I think they plan to leave me up on the moors for the Beast. I'm going to be the main course.' It all clicked into place.

Faisal was almost sick on the floor. 'But how would they know where to leave you? The Beast could be anywhere.'

'It would have to have the scent of me . . . and I think it does.' I looked round them. 'When I first arrived they took my clothes, I think they've used them to give the Beast my scent.' Hadn't I suspected that all week? 'Anyway, if they left me up there, they would just say I'd run off again – wouldn't matter if the Beast got me or not . . . as long as I was dead, and eventually identified as Noel. And there's always the Moorshap Mire.' I shivered at the thought of being swallowed down into its murky depths. 'They win either way.'

Noel nodded. 'Sounds just like them. No one outside would believe how scary they are. How evil. They seem so nice and ordinary.'

Kirsten went on. 'Anyway, *Hansel and Gretel* had a happy ending. Gretel saved the day. And they turned the tables on the witch.'

I liked that. I looked at Noel. 'That's what we're going to do – turn the tables on Aunt Mary and Uncle William. I'm going to get away, and, with Faisal and Kirsten's help, you're going to have them arrested and take your rightful place. Happy ending all round.'

But no ending for me, I thought. Just another beginning.

48

Kirsten glanced out of the window. 'Mr Darling's coming. Get Noel out of here.'

Noel didn't have to be told twice. He grabbed the last of his sandwich, hurried into the bike shed. 'Don't forget about me.' He grinned. Not afraid – excited. He'd kept himself out of the clutches of Aunt Mary and Uncle William too long to be afraid.

'As if,' I said.

We were all sitting at our desks, reading, when the teacher came back. That in itself must have looked suspicious. 'I've decided to send you home early,' he said. 'I've called your families. They'll be here shortly.' He looked out at the snow. 'Might come to nothing, but you're better safe at home in weather like this.'

Safe at home. Neither me nor Noel would be safe there.

Mr Darling looked at Kirsten. 'Afraid I couldn't get any answer at your house. But you can stay here with Mrs Darling and me until your mother comes for you.'

Kirsten hesitated, thinking things through. 'Couldn't I go home with Faisal?' she said suddenly.

Faisal almost fell off his chair.

'My mum could pick me up from his house.'

I was amazed at how quickly Kirsten could come up with ideas. She fluttered her eyelashes at the teacher. Yes . . . I was sure she fluttered her eyelashes. 'And I really want to apologise for everything to Faisal and his family.' She left her desk and walked up to the teacher. She bent close and whispered. I glanced at Faisal. He looked really worried. What was Kirsten up to now?

Mr Darling listened incredulously. 'You've got a crush on Faisal?' He repeated what Kirsten had just told him. His voice as much of a whisper as hers.

'That's why I've been so nasty to him. He doesn't bother with me, Mr Darling.'

No wonder, the teacher thought, *the way you've been treating him*.

'If I could go home with him today it would give me a chance to make it up to him. Apologise to his lovely family.'

He knew Faisal's dad liked Kirsten, got on well with her father. Not her mother. But then, who could get on with her mother?

'We'll see what his dad says when he comes, Kirsten. He might not want that. His decision, OK?'

I had wondered how we would get Uncle William to come into the school and give Faisal a chance to get Noel into the boot of his car. I needn't have worried. The problem was solved for me.

212

I heard the car arriving just as Mr Darling's mobile began to ring. He answered it and I saw his body relax. He even smiled a little. He looked at me as he clicked off the phone. He held up his hand. 'Hold on, I want your uncle to hear this too, Noel. I've just had some news from my wife,' he said. He walked to the door of the schoolhouse and beckoned Uncle William inside.

He looked puzzled, but came without a word.

All the time my heart was roaring. This wasn't some unknown boy we were smuggling into the car. This was the real Noel Christie. If Uncle William saw him, recognised him, then what? Would it matter? Not to Noel. The truth would come out. But it would matter to me.

I had to make sure Uncle William didn't see Noel. Not yet.

Uncle William stood at the door, barring Faisal's way.

'Can I go and look for my dad, sir?' Faisal said. He was eager to warn his dad about Kirsten. His job too was to get Noel into the boot.

'Not yet, Faisal. In a moment.' The teacher looked at Uncle William. 'I've had a call from my wife. It's just been on the news. The Beast has been found. Dead.'

Aunt Mary sat in the chair, shaking. She'd heard it on the radio and couldn't believe it. The Beast was dead. Just their rotten luck. It had been found a few hours ago. All their wonderful plans up in the air again. If only William was here, and she wondered if he'd heard the news too. He probably had, on the car radio. Thank goodness for William. Knowing her wonderful husband, he would already have an alternative plan.

'Did you say the Beast was a puma, sir?' I asked.

'Yes, according to the report, an exceptionally large puma. They've just found the body. But what wonderful news. It's dead at last.'

Faisal was ready to run out of the door. 'Can I go and watch for my dad now, sir? I want to be the first to tell him.'

Mr Darling smiled. 'Of course you can, Faisal. All safe now.'

Faisal brushed past Uncle William. He was staring at me in shock. The Beast was dead. Nothing to eat me now, he must be thinking! I wondered what he intended for me instead.

'I don't think it's such good news,' Kirsten said. 'The poor thing. Murdered. Dead. Seems such a shame.'

'It has killed someone on the moors. A boy,' Mr Darling reminded her.

'We don't know that,' she said at once. 'Someone else could have killed him and left his body for the Beast.' She watched Uncle William when she said that.

I saw him start and wished she'd kept her mouth shut. It was too near the truth for Uncle William. He turned his blue-eyed gaze on her.

'But I suppose we don't want that to happen to anyone else, do we, Mr Christie?' she said sweetly.

Mr Christie was finding it very hard to speak. 'I'm sure we don't,' he said.

But the Beast wasn't dead. I knew that. A puma, I was thinking. It wasn't a puma I had seen. There was still a Beast on the moors.

He knew he had to get off before the snow grew heavier. He couldn't risk blocked roads holding him up. The woman talked too much, wanted company. It was hard to get away from her. Now he was in his room, packed up and ready to go. He had had his message answered. Orders to move on. The Dark Man stood at the window, watching. The pupils were being sent home early. He saw the Christie man arrive, saw him stride into the school, beckoned by the teacher at the door.

The Dark Man was ready to turn away when a movement caught his eye. He turned back. The boot of Christie's car had been opened. The boy, Faisal, was there. He looked furtive. The only way to describe the way he glanced up and down the driveway, watching in case anyone saw him. The boy's eyes scanned towards the window and the Dark Man drew back into the shadows of the room.

What was the boy up to? He glanced out again and could see a door open behind Faisal, the door to some kind of shed that was attached to the school. A figure emerged; he couldn't see who it was. Hidden behind the car, all he could make out was a movement.

What was going on?

His heart leapt. The figure was a boy. There was a flash of clothes, a foot kicking against the car, and the boy was in the boot. It was slammed down by this Faisal.

He looked round again, guiltily. The Dark Man watched as he knocked on the boot twice – a signal. Then he hurried back into the school.

There was a boy hidden in the boot of that car. A boy who'd obviously been hiding in the shed.

A boy on the run.

He'd found him again. He was sure of it.

49

'I'll see you all on Monday,' Mr Darling told us. There was relief in his voice. The Beast was dead. At least everyone thought so. I wanted to tell Faisal and Kirsten otherwise, but there was no time.

You won't see me, I thought, *because on Monday I'll be gone.* And Noel? Where would Noel be?

Faisal came running into the classroom. He looked happy. Winked at me. Noel was safely in the boot, that wink was saying. 'Still no sign of my dad. But he'll be here any time.'

Uncle William had waited long enough. 'Noel and I will be getting along.'

He was eager to go. Mr Darling looked from him to me. Could he see that Uncle William's mind was on other things? Could he read my mind, read that there was no way I'd be here on Monday?

Uncle William had no intention of me being here either. Did he think I didn't know that? Well, both Noel and I had a surprise for him.

The Dark Man was ready to leave, took one last look out

of the window. The nephew, Noel, was in the car now too. He could see his red jacket. Did he know about the boy in the boot? Bet he did. They were all in it together. He could see it all. The boy hides in the shed, the pupils find him, decide to hide him there. He had been metres from him all this time! The boy was resourceful, he had to admit that. He almost admired him. Now the pupils were moving him on to the Christie's house perhaps. An adventure to them. A tragedy for the boy in the boot.

He watched the car as it turned back on to the road. Well, he would follow them to the cottage and find the boy alone.

Better alone.

Faisal's dad fussed about Kirsten coming home with them.

Faisal and Kirsten assured him Mrs Stewart would approve. 'Come on, Dad,' Faisal said. 'It's not the first time Kirsten's been picked up at our house.'

Mr Darling wondered why suddenly Faisal was so up for it. They were up to something these two. And he thought again, *Thank heaven it's Friday*.

Faisal's dad was afraid of Kirsten's mum. The teacher was sure of it. And he didn't blame him. She was one spikey female. But he could see that Faisal was getting annoyed at his fussy little dad. Finally, his dad gave in. Kirsten, spikey as her mother, ploughed in.

'I will take complete responsibility,' she said. 'If my mum says anything, I will tell her it was my decision.'

Faisal dragged his rucksack behind him as they walked to the car. Kirsten bounced past him. She'd got her way, as usual.

Mr Darling tried to assure Mr Yusaf. 'Kirsten's gone to your house before. I'm sure it will be OK.'

Mr Yusaf didn't look reassured. 'Yes, but you never know which way that woman is going to jump.' His eyes followed Kirsten, watched as she hauled Faisal from the front seat so she could sit there. 'A bit like her daughter.'

Mr McGuffin came out then too. He looked in a hurry. Mr Darling waved a farewell to him, but couldn't help thinking he was glad to see him go.

🏃

Faisal saw Mr McGuffin coming towards him. Towards *him*. He was smiling. 'I'm off now. Haven't had a chance to get to know you at all.' His glance hardly took in Kirsten sitting snootily in the front seat. She ignored him.

'Going home early, eh?'

Faisal was dying to tell him about all the excitement. He was sure Mr McGuffin was the kind of man who would understand . . . help even.

'Yes, going home. Did you hear they've caught the Beast?'

'Killed it,' Kirsten said without even looking.

'So all your excitement's over now,' Mr McGuffin said.

And Faisal couldn't help answering. 'Oh, I wouldn't say that. We've still got things happening . . .'

Kirsten swivelled in her seat, snapped at him. 'Faisal. Get in the car!' She sounded like a nagging wife. She

219

sounded just like his mother when she bossed his dad about.

'Things happening . . . like what?'

Faisal could still see in his mind Mr McGuffin struggling with Wilkie. He was a hero. A fighter. He was like someone out of the movies. *Bet he could help us*, he was thinking. But Kirsten shouted at him again. Glared at him, as if she could see how tempted he was to tell him everything.

He got in the back of the car, shrugging his shoulders. Mr McGuffin stood at the door as if he was waiting. But the moment was gone. Faisal wouldn't say anything now.

Faisal watched his dad heading for the car. How small he looked compared to Mr McGuffin. He tried not to think like that. Felt as if he was betraying his dad, but he couldn't stop thinking it. Mr McGuffin moved off at last. Kirsten turned to him. 'What is he after? You almost told him everything.'

'He could help us, I'm sure of it. I think he likes me,' Faisal said. 'Sees me as the son he never had.'

Kirsten smirked. 'Ha! Well, I don't trust him. I'm glad it's Friday. And he's gone. Paul's safe, and I've just figured out how we're going to help Ram get away.'

It was the first Faisal had heard about this. 'How's that then?'

'Abdullah's van. The Resistance. We helped Paul that way, didn't we?'

'Yeah . . .'

'Well, we're going to use the Resistance to help Ram escape too.'

50

Uncle William said nothing on the way home, and neither did I. I had too much on my mind. I kept praying he had no intention of dumping me somewhere out here now. But it was still light. I had a feeling he would wait till it was dark. But what was his plan now that the Beast had been killed? I had my own plans. I was leaving tonight, one way or another, across the moors. I would never know the outcome of our little scheme – I only hoped, for all our sakes, it would work. If it did, it would be just revenge on them all. I knew the puma they had found was not the Beast. I remembered then the shot I had heard the other night. The man with the rifle. I'd bet it was him who had shot the puma. And they had only just discovered the body. But somewhere up there on the moors, there was still the Beast.

Let the snow come down, and the fog.

Tonight, I was out of here. Away from this madness.

The cottage appeared, warm and welcoming, like some old-fashioned ideal of home. There was a light shining in a downstairs room, in the kitchen – Aunt Mary cooking again. Feeding me up, one last time, for the Beast. Probably had the meal ready before she heard

221

the sad news. The Beast was dead but she wasn't going to let a good meal go to waste, was she?

Uncle William pulled to a halt outside the front door. I looked at him. 'Aren't you going into the garage?'

Uncle William smiled. 'Not tonight. Have to go out again later.' I stepped out of the car. He didn't look back as I clipped open the boot and tapped on it gently. Noel would have to get himself hidden in the garage while I kept them occupied.

I hurried into the kitchen as soon as I went in. Aunt Mary was at the stove. I sniffed appreciatively. 'Something smells good,' I said. I lifted the lid of the pot, looked inside. Stew. Rich with thick gravy and vegetables. I'd been right. I knew it then. She'd had the meal ready before the news of the Beast's death had reached her. Poor soul.

I began gushing to her and Uncle William about the Beast, and how we didn't have to worry any more. We could go walking in the hills; I could spend time outside the school. Hardly knew what I was talking about. I was keeping them occupied. That was all. Finally, I had nothing else to say. If Noel wasn't out of that boot by now, he'd never get out. I stood for a moment, looking slightly lost.

Then I held up my rucksack. 'Better get my homework done, eh?' I said and I hurried upstairs. From my window I could see the garage. The door lay slightly ajar. Noel was inside by now. I was sure of it.

I emptied my rucksack of school books and stuffed it with the clothes from the wardrobe. Noel's clothes. I was sure he wouldn't mind. He had plenty of money to buy more. I'd grab food from the kitchen too. I didn't intend to go hungry again for a while.

There was the book on the pile by my bedside. *Hansel and Gretel*. Now I knew what the story was about I felt cold inside. Had that really been what they were doing? Fattening me up for the Beast?

But this wasn't a story. This was life. My life. On the run. No one to trust. I needed to remember my past. What was keeping me from remembering?

The Dark Man was here. I could still feel him close. What did he want from me? What did I know that scared him so much?

For a moment I sat on the bed, laid low with fear and misery. I was surrounded by evil, it seemed to me. Always afraid, never knowing what to do next. No one knowing and no one caring.

And the thought came to me again . . . Why was no one looking for me?

The Dark Man parked a distance from the cottage, trained his binoculars on the battered old car in the driveway. The boot was lying slightly ajar. He could make out in the snow light footsteps heading for the garage. It wasn't rocket science to figure out that he was hiding there. He would wait here till it was dark, till the house lay in silence. He would make sure the boy didn't leave. He wouldn't lose him this time. This time there must be no mistakes.

Now he knew that the boy had been under his nose all this time, he could even manage a smile at the audacity of it. The boy always seemed to find friends to help him.

But this time he would not escape.

At Faisal's house Kirsten eventually had a chance to explain her plan. That was only after she had apologised to Auntie Furzana, Auntie Munan, Granny and Faisal's mother. Even so, their faces were unsmiling. No amount of apologising was going to make them totally forgive her. Only after all this were they allowed to go to Faisal's room on the pretext of doing some homework.

There Kirsten made him call his cousin and tell him to bring the van back to Noel's house that night. From there they would get Ram into the van and away to safety. She had it all figured out.

Abdullah wasn't very happy about it. He had a date. He was celebrating his first successful mission, he said.

'Definitely as daft as you,' Kirsten muttered.

Although, in fact, Kirsten had to admit that Abdullah had been particularly brilliant. He had taken Paul to a friend's house when they had got to town. Abdullah and his pals were doing a sponsored cycle to the next town, and alongside them, Paul had cycled his way to freedom. 'He's hiding with another cousin of ours now,' Abdullah had told them. 'He says he'll keep in touch.'

Paul, safe – it made her feel good. He would never be in danger again.

Reluctantly, Abdullah finally agreed to give up his date. But only because, like Faisal, the idea of helping the Resistance appealed to him.

'This better not be going to spoil Operation Noel,' Faisal said.

'Well, of course it won't. This is only going to make it easier for him to get away.'

Faisal didn't want to appear eager to agree with Kirsten too quickly. 'So how do we let Ram know this plan of yours?' he asked her.

'We phone him, bonehead.'

He decided that if she called him 'bonehead' one more time he was going to thump her. Girl or not. Honestly, who would have blamed him?

Kirsten dialled the number on her mobile. It was answered by Aunt Mary. Kirsten put on her poshest voice. 'Hello, Mrs Christie? It's Kirsten here. Can I speak to Noel, please?'

Faisal put his head close to Kirsten's so he could listen. There was a hesitation, then a voice, still with that chilling smile in it. 'I'm afraid he went to bed early, dear. Had a headache. Don't want to disturb him.'

The phone clicked off before she could say another word. Kirsten looked at Faisal. 'Went to bed! I don't think so.'

'Do you think they've done something already? Maybe we should call the police!'

Kirsten was determined they wouldn't do that. 'Ram wouldn't let that happen. He has to get away. He doesn't want the police involved.'

'So, what now?'

Kirsten thought for only a moment. 'We'll have to go to the house. Get him ourselves. Sneak him out of there somehow.' She sat on the bed thoughtfully. 'Course, first we've got to get some transport.'

It was Faisal's turn for a bright idea. 'My bikes!'

I was coming downstairs and saw Aunt Mary put the phone down. 'Dinner ready soon,' she said.

'Who was that?' I asked, trying to sound innocent.

'Wrong number,' was all she said.

The smell of the stew wafted through the house. Gravy, dumplings, mashed potatoes – a feast fit for a king. 'I made your favourite,' she said.

And the condemned man ate a hearty meal, I thought. My last meal. I knew that's what it was. Maybe she had made my favourite with some crazy idea of doing something nice for me before they sent me to my death. She was insane enough to think that.

Well, I would eat her hearty meal. It would keep me going for the night ahead.

Noel shivered in the garage. He wasn't cold, he was excited. He looked forward to the night ahead, to what he had to do. Operation Noel. His revenge at last.

My aim was to leave after dinner – pretend I was going to bed, and be out of the window and away before the alarm was set.

Uncle William had his own plans too.

'I have to go out after dinner, Noel. I'd like you to come with me.'

'It's safe now they've caught the Beast,' Aunt Mary said.

So this was their plan for me, then, going into action. I was sure it had to be. He was planning to take me somewhere remote, leave me there – either dead already, or, more likely, unconscious. But I had to get away from this house; that was part of Operation Noel too. So I decided to go along with him. I would let him take me in the car. And once we were clear of the house, I would get away from him somehow. If I had to struggle for the keys, if it meant I had to leap from a moving car, I would get out of that car and go.

'So where are we going exactly?' I said.

Uncle William pretended not to hear.

I didn't ask again.

51

'Right, we're out of here, Faisal. Synergise watches.'

'It's synchronise, Kirsten, and stop talking like a detective!' She was really getting up his nose.

'We have to help Ram escape. There's no time to lose.'

'We have to escape from my aunties first,' he reminded her.

His Auntie Furzana caught them at the front door. 'Where are you two going?' she asked. Her arms folded, standing above them like some fabled genie.

'We're going out for a breath of fresh air, Auntie,' Faisal said.

'You'll do no such thing. You'll stay inside. There's a monster out there.'

'It's been shot, Auntie,' Faisal reminded her.

'It could have a friend,' she said at once.

At the back door, it was his auntie Munan who was on guard duty, sitting like a Buddha, her feet in a basin of hot water. 'And where do you think you two are going?!' she asked.

His granny was waiting at the door of the utility room, watching the washing doing its final spin. 'Her favourite hobby,' Faisal whispered to Kirsten.

'You can't go out on a night like this,' she said. 'Stay indoors. Keep warm. Here is some Turkish delight.' She knew her grandson couldn't resist that.

'I don't believe this!' Kirsten said as they were turned away from there too. 'Your aunties and granny should have been guards at Colditz. No one would ever have escaped from there then. Are there any other ways out of this house, Faisal?'

Faisal thought about that. 'We could climb out of the bathroom window. There's a ledge outside that lets us down to the back of the house.' He shook his head. 'Though how I'm going to explain being in the bathroom with you I don't know.'

'How *you're* going to explain!' Kirsten was already pulling him on.

But for once they found a room in the house that was empty – for the moment at least. In they went and locked the door. Faisal opened the window, looked outside. It seemed a lot further from the ground than he remembered. 'Do you think you'll manage to jump down there, Kirsten?'

She almost had him out of the window head first when he said that.

'Who do you think you're talking to?' she snapped at Faisal. 'Just you go out first and if you fall, at least I can land on you.'

Faisal might have laughed if he hadn't thought she was serious. He climbed out and stepped on to the ledge. Kirsten was at the window, urging him on. 'Hurry up and jump. We haven't got all night.'

Faisal closed his eyes and leapt. He landed with a thud, but kept his feet. Then he looked up. 'OK, smartie. Hurry up and jump.'

He half hoped she would freeze on the ledge, plead for help, beg him to come up and get her. In his dreams. Kirsten was standing beside him in a moment.

'The bikes are round here,' Faisal said. 'You can ride a bike, can't you?'

Kirsten looked at him as if he was mad.

They pushed the bikes up the driveway and on to the road. One glance behind assured them that no one in the house had been alerted so far.

'This is mad,' Faisal muttered. 'The Beast could get us.'

Kirsten tutted. 'It's dead, remember?'

But Faisal was worried that perhaps his auntie was right. Maybe it had a friend.

It was dark now, with flakes of snow falling silently. The Dark Man stayed back in the shadows, waiting for the moment when the lights would go off in the house and he could find the boy in the garage. He had crept close to the house to wait. He felt as if he could almost smell his prey, he was so close.

The front door of the cottage opened, sending a stream of light on to the path. William Christie appeared, pulling on a heavy overcoat. The Dark Man sank back into the shelter of the trees.

William Christie called back into the house. 'Come on, Noel.'

The nephew was going with him. Good. There would only be the woman left. He'd have a free hand to get the boy. He pressed his back against the tree, heard car doors open, and then slam shut. The engine purred into life, moved off. He stepped further back into the shadows as the car came his way. His vision was blurred by the branches of a tree and the snow and the darkness.

What made him look? He'd never know. A man seldom taken by surprise, he was surprised now. Shocked.

The nephew was sitting in the passenger seat, staring straight ahead, face grim. The Dark Man could have sworn in the second it took for the car to pass that he recognised that profile.

The boy.

Gone in an instant. Yet in that instant he'd been sure.

Couldn't be. That boy in the red jacket was Noel Christie, William Christie's nephew, attending school with the other pupils.

It had to be his imagination. Searching for the boy, thinking about him, obsessed with finding him.

He'd made a mistake. It had been a trick of the light. He had only seen him through a blur of falling snow.

No. He'd find the boy he wanted, hiding in the garage.

52

'Are you sure Abdullah knows the right house to go to?' Kirsten called back to him.

'How many times have I got to tell you, Kirsten? Abdullah knows this area like the back of his hand.'

'I take it the brains all went to his side of the family, then?'

He was about to answer her when something flew past him, brushed against his hair, sending him tumbling from his bike. He yelled.

Kirsten turned and stopped. 'What's wrong now?'

'Something tried to get me.' He knew the Beast had been killed, no danger from there, he had to admit. But there were other things to threaten them. Bats, foxes, wolves maybe. 'I think it was a bat.'

No sympathy from Kirsten. She just stood and glared at him. 'Get on your bike. This is no time to play games.'

'Hope the next bat gets you,' he whispered, but not quite loud enough for her to hear. And then he clambered back on his bike and peddled like mad after her.

The Dark Man pushed open the door of the garage and slipped inside, listening for any sound, the least sound. Alert for the slightest stirring in the shadows. He heard nothing. Saw nothing.

But someone was in here. That much he knew. There was only one way into the garage, and one way out. Whoever was in here was trapped.

He took a step forward, his keen eyes searching in every corner. At last he caught a movement. Something hidden under boxes and blankets and cases. He leapt forward, snatched off the blanket. There was a figure in there, ready to leap away from him. A boy. He grabbed him by the shoulders. 'I've got you at last.'

The boy struggled. Of course he struggled. He knew what was going to happen. But he wouldn't let him go. He hauled him to the light from the door, a single beam of light. The boy was fighting, struggling, swearing.

The Dark Man gripped him even tighter, drew in an angry breath when he saw his face. A face he did not recognise. 'Who are you?' He shook him angrily.

The boy retorted boldly, 'Who are you?!'

The Dark Man's mind was a rollercoaster of thoughts. He didn't understand how it had happened, didn't know what was going on. No time to think of it. Because he realised now he'd been right in the first place.

The boy in the car, the boy they were passing off as Noel Christie was the one he was after. Who this boy was didn't matter.

He threw him from him. The boy stumbled back, kept his feet, called after him angrily. But the Dark Man didn't hear. The Dark Man was gone.

53

'We're doing an awful stupid thing,' Faisal said.

The further along this dark and lonely road they cycled the eerier it became. The Christie's cottage was the last on the road. After that there was nothing but desolate moorland. Was that why Aunt Mary and Uncle William had chosen to move here? Faisal wondered.

'We're doing the only thing we can to help Ram.' Kirsten was breathless. 'We're getting him out of here.' Her words were caught by a gust of snow, whipped past his ears in a second. 'Do you think the Resistance was worried about a little thing like danger? And we're not going to be shot at dawn if we're caught,' she reminded him again.

No, Faisal thought, *but we might be eaten by sunrise*.

Because no matter what they said about the Beast being dead, Faisal still felt there was something out there, keeping pace with them, watching them, ready to pounce at any moment.

My heart was beating fast. I kept glancing his way, waiting for the moment. I knew this was it – the time was approaching when he planned to kill me. We were driving up towards the moors. I had been prepared since the minute I got into the car. I fingered the can of de-icer I'd pushed down the side of my seat. It wasn't much of a weapon, but it was better than nothing. He was taking me here for a sinister purpose. But I had a purpose too.

I was prepared to leap from the car at any moment. The child lock would be on, but if I could get the window down, I could open the door from the outside. Or I might even leap through the window. My hands were shaking. I could see them shaking on my lap. He hadn't said a word, this Uncle William – kept his eyes fixed on the road all the time he was driving, as if he was psyching himself up for what was ahead.

My body was tense but I was not afraid. I'd been in tight spots before – somehow it seemed natural, this ability to think straight in times of crisis. I had to keep calm. Uncle William was mad. Him and his wife. I saw that clearly now. Maybe separately they would have gone through life doing nothing wrong. Perhaps people would have thought them just slightly eccentric. But they met up, got together, and that's when sparks began to fly, trouble started. Madness ensued. There was a name for that. I racked my brain to remember what it was . . . couldn't think.

He suddenly swerved from the winding road, and the car bumped on to the rugged path that led up to the moors.

The Beast had been caught. It was dead. That's what everyone thought. I knew different. Knew I could still be its next victim. My mouth was dry as dust, my body tingled. The moment was almost here.

Kirsten's mother had arrived at Faisal's house much later than expected. She was as icy as ever, but there was an edge in her voice that Faisal's dad couldn't help but notice. He was always a little nervous with Mrs Stewart, but especially tonight. All that nonsense about his Faisal bullying Kirsten. Ha! His son bully Kirsten? How could anyone believe that?

'I was so glad they made up,' he said as he led her inside the house. He knew he was twittering on, couldn't stop himself. 'They seem to be getting on so well tonight. Haven't heard a thing from them since they came in. My wife has gone up to get Kirsten.'

She hardly answered him. She looked as if she had other things on her mind. And for the first time he noticed that her face was drawn. She looked strained. Worry? Stress? She was always working. She should spend more time with her family, he thought.

His wife came rushing into the living room. Bright spots on her face, her eyes wide with alarm. 'They've gone.' Her voice was breathless. 'They've both gone.'

'Those naughty children.' He leapt to his feet, punched in a number on the phone. 'Faisal's mobile,' he explained. 'They're probably just outside somewhere.'

He looked up after a moment. 'He's switched it off.'

Kirsten's mother was already on her phone to her daughter. Her face had drained to grey. She held the phone to her ear and Faisal's dad saw her hand was shaking. 'N-nothing,' she said. 'Hers is switched off too.'

Faisal's dad dared to put a hand out to her. A bold move considering he was terrified of the woman. 'They've been cooped up for so long, never getting out of doors. They just want a bit of freedom.' He smiled reassuringly at her. 'There's nothing to worry about now. The Beast is dead.'

And all at once, the ice-cool blonde was crying. Her eyes bubbled with tears. She clutched at his hand as if she needed him to comfort her. He was embarrassed, but more than that, amazed.

'But that's where you're wrong . . . there's everything to worry about. The Beast isn't dead. We have to find them. Now!'

The Dark Man followed the tracks of the car in the snow, saw the swerve of tyres turning on to the dirt road. Where were they going? What was happening? How had the boy fooled the man into believing he was his nephew? He couldn't understand. Couldn't work it out at all. The boy was clever, he had to give him that. What devious plan had he come up with now? The boy had been here all this time, so close, and he had not known it.

But he knew it now.

Uncle William's car drew to a halt. Outside black as ink all around us, just a smattering of snow falling against the windscreen.

'Here, put this on.' He handed me Jake's coat. Jake's coat. I was never so glad to see anything. Part of the little past I had. Part of my memory. I grabbed it from him, shoved my arms in the sleeves, wrapped it round me. I hardly knew why he was bothering to give it back to me. If he thought the Beast was dead, what was the point of me wearing something full of my scent? But then, Uncle William was mad. Maybe he hoped there might be something else out there, just as hungry.

He turned to me. 'We're here.' It was pitch-black and his face was reflected in the green and red lights from the dashboard. He had never been more frightening than he was at that moment.

'We're here – where?' Because we were nowhere.

'The end of the road,' he said. There was no smile now. Only menace. 'For you anyway, Noel . . . or whoever you are.'

I tugged at the door.

'Child lock, remember?' he said, smiling.

'Aren't you a bit late? The Beast is dead. Nothing to eat me now.' I needed time to think, wanted him to talk. He wasn't fooled.

'Worked something out, have you?' If he was surprised he didn't show it. 'Doesn't matter. Let's just say . . . you've served your purpose.'

Did he think it was going to be this easy? No way. Not with this boy. He took the keys out of the ignition, and in that instant I put my plan into action. I lifted the de-icer and sprayed it right into his eyes. He yelled angrily, dropped the keys. I grabbed them, pressed the unlock button for the door and leapt from the car. He would be after me in a second. I wasted no time. I began to run. I flung the keys as far away as possible, didn't even hear them land. But at least he couldn't drive after me. I scrabbled up through the moors and the moss. Didn't know where I was going. Just away from Uncle William.

Then I heard it, and it made me stop in my tracks. Wailing through the snow and the mist. The howl of the Beast.

54

They had reached the Christies' cottage. They stayed on the road as Kirsten stepped from her bike quietly. Faisal fell off his. Kirsten turned on him in annoyance. 'We have to be quiet!' She hauled him behind a stone dyke, just before Aunt Mary pulled a curtain across the window and looked outside.

'Don't even breathe,' Kirsten said, walloping a hand across Faisal's mouth. He felt like biting it. Why did she have to be so bossy?

They waited till Aunt Mary had moved away from the window before they stepped from behind the darkness of the dyke. The air hung thick with silence.

'Ram said Noel will be in the garage. Come on.' They crept quietly towards the old wooden building, and Kirsten pushed open the door silently. 'Noel?' she said softly.

Faisal was startled by the figure that appeared from the dark shadows. He thought it was Ram. The same height, the same dark hair. For a fleeting moment, they really did look alike.

'We've come for Ram,' Kirsten said. 'We're going to help him get away from here.'

Faisal was determined she wasn't going to be doing all the talking. 'My cousin's coming back with his van. We're going to hide him in there, just the way we did with Paul. He'll take him to safety.'

'Just like the Resistance,' Kirsten said proudly.

Noel shook his head. 'You're too late. He's not here. He went off with Uncle William.'

Too late! No, Kirsten wouldn't have that. 'We have to catch up with them.'

'We didn't pass them on the road,' Faisal said. 'So they must have gone the other way –'

Kirsten finished his sentence. 'The other way that takes them up into the most desolate part of the moor?' She sounded afraid. Faisal knew she was thinking what he was. This was it – what William Christie had planned for him all the time.

'Why did he go off with him? Why didn't he run away?' Kirsten sounded angry about that.

'I don't think he had a lot of choice,' Noel said.

Faisal took her arm. 'We'll go after them, Kirsten. We'll find him. He can't kill all three of us.' Faisal thought for a moment. 'Maybe it's time for us to phone the police.'

'No!' Kirsten said at once. 'If we bring the police into this, it'll all come out. Paul won't be safe, Noel won't be safe and what about Ram? The Dark Man could find him.'

Noel suddenly gasped, remembering. 'The Dark Man . . . ? He was here. He thought I was Ram . . . he's gone after him too.'

Faisal pulled at Kirsten. 'Oh no! Come on! No time

to waste.'

Kirsten looked at Noel. 'What about you? Will you be OK?'

Noel smiled. 'I'm just about to put Ram's plan into operation.'

Uncle William was after me. I could hear him close in on me as I ran; hear his feet slide and scrabble on the mossy rocks. He needed me dead. His plan was to leave me in some cleft of rock – his nephew, Noel, a boy with a history of running away, who had run away once too often. He would leave me dead or unconscious, or maybe make sure I was sucked into the mire.

And if the Beast got me . . . so much the better.

And there was still a Beast. I had known it all day. What I had seen had been no puma, not even one larger than any reported before.

But the howl had scared the hell out of me. It was here, somewhere, and it was too close. It had the scent of me. I was wearing Jake's coat, and they had used my clothes to lay a scent around the moors. Must have done. It was all becoming clear as I ran.

I was lost. The night was so black, so frightening, and a deadly mire, the Moorshap, lay all around me. I stopped for a second to catch my breath, looked behind me. I could see nothing. Shapes shifting through the fog and the snow, that was all. But I knew he was still there. He would never give up till he got me. There was madness in his eyes.

I took a step forward and my foot sank deep into the

mire, felt it being sucked down. I plucked my foot free, fell back, afraid. One wrong step and I would be history.

Faisal's dad still couldn't take it in. 'The Beast has not been killed . . . that's what you're saying.'

Kirsten's mother was still crying. 'Yes, still alive, still up on the moors. And it's all my fault.'

They had phoned the police, but she itched to be doing something. 'I just can't stand around here waiting.'

Faisal's dad was still trying to take it in. 'No ordinary animal,' she had said. 'A creature we created at the research facility. I helped to create her. Mixing genes, making her stronger, more vicious.'

'But why?' Faisal's mother was crying too.

'We told ourselves it was to discover new ways to cure diseases, but really it was because we could. There are other things going on in that facility. Experiments that should be stopped. It's time it was closed.' She sobbed then. Hard, gut-wrenching sobs.

'This is no time for crying!' Mr Yusaf said, taking himself by surprise, talking to her as if she was a child. But he was frightened now. Frightened for his son.

She looked at him, took a deep breath and went on. 'Then she escaped. No one knows quite how. At first we hoped we could recapture her . . . but we had made her clever too. So clever she couldn't be hunted down. We hired a man to kill her, thought for a day or two that he had. But it was a puma he killed.' She paused. 'It was a puma they found today. A big puma. One of ours, of

243

course. But not the Beast.' She sunk her head in her hands and began crying again. 'My whole life's falling apart. It's a judgement on me.'

Faisal's dad stood up. 'They've taken the bikes – can't have gone far. We'll go after them in your car.'

She was glad to be doing something. Followed him meekly.

The Dark Man had found Christie's car, parked at the end of a dirt path. The doors were open as if someone had left it too quickly. The boy. He had run away from Christie – this man who had pretended he was his uncle. He could picture it now. The boy leaping from the car and running . . . where?

He let the headlights of his car pick out the footprints on the track heading for the moorland – dangerous place to go. The boy was running. Quick light footprints, the man seconds behind him. There was anger in the deep prints he made as he ran after him.

What had happened here? Why was Christie after the boy? He didn't know, but it would take more than a mad uncle to kill this boy.

He stepped from the car and looked up into the blackness of the moor. Somewhere up there was his prey.

He began to climb.

55

I was afraid of everything. Here in the dark, trying to find the right step to take, a safe way to move forward. Listening for the madman behind me, listening for the least sound – a step, a breath, a growl. Waiting for something to leap at me . . . man or beast. My heart roared with fear. This was the Moorshap, where bodies went down and down and were gone for ever.

No one would miss me. No one would care. I didn't matter to anyone.

Yet, I had to survive. I didn't know why, but there had to be a reason.

My mind swirled. I was somewhere else. Somewhere else that was dark, and just as terrifying.

'You have it. The proof. Use it. Stop it. It's up to you now.'

Where had that voice come from? What did it mean? The proof? What proof? I clawed at my ears as if I could pull more of the memory out of my head.

That whispered, desperate voice. *'You have the proof.'*

'Noel.' Uncle William's voice suddenly burst through the darkness, and the memory was gone. He was calling me still by the only name he knew. 'Noel, you little monster. I'm coming to get you.'

I wanted to call back to him. 'Never!' But I wouldn't give away my location. He was too close behind me. And I had one consolation.

If I was lost, so was he.

Faisal and Kirsten had followed the tracks in the lightly falling snow, found not one, but two cars at the bottom of the murky path. 'They're both after him,' Kirsten said. 'How scared he must be.' She looked at Faisal. 'We have to save him.' She said it as if Faisal was going to disagree with her. No wonder she got up his nose.

'I know we have to save him!' he said. 'But how? He might be dead already.'

He didn't want to think that but it had to be faced.

Kirsten would not hear of such a thing. 'No. We're going to find him alive. We're going to save him. There has to be a reason he has to live. He must have some big secret in that memory of his. We're going to make sure he gets away.'

'When did you stop being such an annoying little madam, and turn into . . .'

Faisal couldn't bring himself to say what he was thinking. When had she turned into a warrior queen, a fighter, a tower of strength?

In the dark, he could see her smile. She supplied the perfect word . . . 'A heroine!' she said smugly. Then her smile disappeared. 'Come on, bonehead, or it will be morning.'

Kirsten's mother drove slowly along the road, following the bicycle tracks through the snow. All the while she kept muttering over and over, 'If anything has happened to them, it'll be all my fault.'

Faisal's dad was too worried to disagree with her. He was angry as well. 'You create this . . . superbeast, and then you let it escape! Why didn't you let the authorities know what they were really looking for? Then the whole area would have been evacuated, helicopters brought in. No boy would have been torn apart on the moor. None of this would have happened if the authorities had been told the truth.'

'I know. I know,' was all she said.

She screamed as she saw the tyre tracks turn from the road. They were near the Christie cottage. Though she'd never been there, they all knew it had been rented recently by the man and woman and their nephew. 'They must have gone to visit that boy. Maybe they're in there with him.'

'No.' Mr Yusaf's eyes already could see the bike tracks come out again. Two bikes. 'They've gone on . . . both of them.' He pointed down the dark road. 'That way . . .' He had taken out his phone. 'I'll call my wife, tell her to let the police know they must have gone into this cottage sometime recently. But they've moved on from here and I'm not wasting time.'

She agreed at once. 'No, neither am I. We'll follow the tracks. But why would they go this way . . . there's nothing out there, but moorland and swamp and . . .' She didn't want to think what was beyond that.

Faisal's dad watched her as she drove. *Not an ice-cool*

247

blonde any more, he thought. *Just a mum worried sick about her little girl.*

'Why are they heading for the moors?' she said again.

🏃

Noel heard the car on the road, heard it come to a halt – engine still running. He hesitated, waited to see if it would turn in here. Was it Uncle William back so soon? He hoped not. That would mean he had dealt with Ram. No, he wouldn't think that way. He wanted Faisal and Kirsten to help Ram. Get him to safety. He peered through a crack in the door of the garage. From there he could make out the car on the road. Definitely not Uncle William's.

After a moment, it moved off – off in the direction of the moors. He looked back to the house. Aunt Mary had heard the car too. The curtain on the bottom window was drawn across. He could almost see her face as she peered outside. Aunt Mary. The last time he'd seen her she'd been screaming.

Soon, she'd be screaming again.

56

The Dark Man had heard the uncle call out, threatening the boy – still calling him Noel. That puzzled him. But the uncle was somewhere nearby. And if he was nearby, so was the boy, and he was still alive. The boy didn't answer. He was too wise to call out an answer. Too clever to give away his position.

The Dark Man stepped forward, not thinking. His foot touched soft ground, too soft. He had heard about the mire. He lifted his foot, stepped to the side. The ground was even softer here. He could feel it cling to his shoe, suck at him hungrily. He took another step, backwards this time, and his foot almost sunk again. Which way to go?

The boy was so close . . . and he couldn't run to get him. Didn't know which way to move.

He was so close, and I couldn't run to get away from him. Didn't know which way to move. Every step I took was mire and swamp. I could hear him coming towards me, hear his footsteps. Could see nothing through the fog and the falling snow. I took a step back, let out a low moan as I hit something solid. Rock. I looked up. A spur of rock hung over me. Loomed above me. I had backed myself into a corner. No way to escape now. Why was there no handy cave for me to slip inside? I wiped the snow from my eyes. Something was moving through the fog; a figure forming from a wisp of mist like something supernatural. Hell-bent on getting me.

And a voice whispered in my mind, '*You can't die. You have the proof. It's all up to you.*'

I felt like calling back, 'You certainly picked the wrong boy for your hero.' Because I was useless.

I began to shake, but I stood tall. I wasn't going down without a fight. I just wished I wasn't so alone.

Kirsten leapt from her bike. 'Two cars.' She looked at Faisal. Uncle William's car door was lying open. She saw in her mind what had happened: Ram pushing open the door, jumping from the car – Mr Christie a second after him. She looked into the fog. They were around somewhere. Up there, where there was the danger of the Moorshap Mire.

She touched the bonnet of the other car. The engine was still warm. 'The Dark Man,' she said.

Faisal left his bike and came over. 'He's after him too. Ram must be terrified.' He looked at the sleek black car, the falling snow melting as it landed on the bonnet. It reminded him of something, he couldn't think what. Kirsten interrupted his thoughts.

'Come on, we're going after them.'

'Up there? That's suicide.'

'No. It's not. I've lived here all my life, Faisal. I know the moors, know the safe route. It was the first thing my mother taught me. She does care sometimes.'

'You know the way even in the dark?'

'We'll take the bike lamps.'

She turned from him and began to climb. Faisal hurried behind her. If she knew where she was going, he wasn't going to lose her.

Aunt Mary peered through the curtains again. Was that another car on the road? Busy tonight. Must be because the Beast had been killed – too early for them. But William was right. There were other dangers on the moors for a runaway boy. The mire, the cliffs, and on a night like this, the freezing cold. A little tap on the head to render him unconscious, William had said, then a little push from a high drop. All completely accidental, of course. And then, just wait for the search parties to find him.

She rehearsed her story exactly as William had told her. Noel had run off again. William had gone off frantically in search of their beloved nephew. Beloved! That was a joke. Noel was never loveable. Should never have been born. William should always have been his brother's heir. Everything they'd done had been forced on them. The car crash that had killed his parents? Well, no one had even questioned that. Except Noel, of course. Everyone had assumed it was a terrible accident. And with Noel orphaned no one had considered anyone else but that the loving brother and his wife would look

251

after him.

They had worked out such a perfect plan. And Noel, of course, had spoiled it.

The little devil had died too soon. It hadn't been her fault he had fallen down those stairs, but who would ever believe that? It had to look like a genuine accident, and he'd made it look like murder. The boy was always difficult.

Anyway, Noel had brought it on himself, claiming they had tampered with the brakes of the car. She had given herself away big time then. It annoyed her still.

She remembered her panic when she couldn't wake him at the bottom of the stairs, and once again, it was her William who calmed her and came up with an alternative plan. They were moving anyway, so why didn't they find someone to impersonate Noel at the new school? It would only be for a few days.

She had been amazed how easy it was to get one of these runaways to come with them on the promise of a great deal of money. Some people were so greedy, she thought. And devious.

Because that one had been as bad as Noel. He had decided that if he was going to be Noel Christie for a while, why couldn't he be Noel Christie for good and get the whole inheritance?

He thought that he could blackmail them because he knew what their plan was. Unfortunately for him, he only knew a part of it. The part he didn't know was that he wasn't meant to get any money at all. He was going to be found on the moors, a victim of the Beast. Wasn't too happy when he discovered that bit. Had tried to run to the police. And, of course, they couldn't let that happen. William had had no choice.

So here was another little devil who had died too soon. Before they had any chance of setting him up as the real Noel.

Honestly, Mary thought bitterly, *children nowadays never do what they're meant to.*

Why, poor William had taken his life in his hands carrying that body up on to the moors.

And even after all this they would still have to go back and get rid of Noel's body. Couldn't leave it in the freezer back at the house in London for ever, unfortunately. It was a wonder, she thought, that after all that she hadn't had a nervous breakdown!

Mary poured herself a cup of tea.

Another sound outside? William back already? No. She hadn't heard his car.

Couldn't be the Beast. The Beast was dead.

She stood up and went to the window again. She pulled the curtain across to look outside.

And screamed.

His face. Close up against the glass. Noel's face. The real Noel. She let go of the curtain and stumbled back, shaking. Afraid.

No.

Had to be her imagination. She'd just been thinking about him. He had been in her mind. She had seen her own reflection, that was all.

She stepped towards the window again, tentatively drew the curtain to one side.

Nothing. There was nothing there, just her own face

staring back at her.

She breathed a sigh of relief. 'Hurry back, William, darling,' she whispered.

Because she was suddenly afraid of being alone here.

57

I could make him out more distinctly now, moving towards me through the fog. It was his eyes I saw most clearly, wide and bright. Mad eyes, and the smile. Still smiling. For ever smiling. He was crazy. They were both crazy.

'I'm going to be so heartbroken,' he was saying, as if he was talking to himself. 'I couldn't find you, no matter how I tried.' He looked down at his shoes, muddy and wet from the swamp; at his clothes, soaked and soiled. 'They'll see how hard I tried. Your poor heartbroken Uncle William. They'll say, "Oh, the poor man. He risked his life going after him."' Then his grin widened and his face looked like a skull in the dusk. 'And I'm your only heir. I'll get all that lovely money at last.'

He looked around. 'I wish I knew exactly where this mire was here. I could just throw you in.' He said it so matter-of-factly, as if it would be nothing to him. He meant it too. 'Then I could leave something of yours lying around here, a shoe perhaps, for the search parties to find. They would drag the swamp, haul you up. Dead, of course. I mean, I couldn't have you down there for ever. It would take years to get the money then. No.

There has to be a body.' He told me this as if it would be some sort of consolation to me. I stepped back. He took a step closer.

I was alone, totally alone. Nowhere to run.

Then I heard it. Just when I thought it was all over, I heard Kirsten scream.

The Dark Man heard it too. Stepping gingerly forward he heard an ear-splitting scream through the fog, close by. But whose? Damn this swamp. His foot sank again. He pulled it free. He would retrace his steps, find another route. He didn't want the boy dead. Not yet. He had to find out what he knew first, but he had no intention of losing him when he was this close.

Someone was coming and Uncle William knew it. Someone was close, here on the moors, and I was saved. I was sure of it. Kirsten and Faisal hopefully coming to my rescue. The sound of that scream gave me heart to go on. I stood tall.

And then he brought out a gun – whisked it from his pocket and pointed it straight at me.

'You can't shoot me!' I said. 'That wouldn't look like an accident.'

He held the gun steady; I heard a click. Was that the safety catch? I realised once again I was staring death in the face.

'Help!' I yelled. Screamed it. Someone had to hear.

Uncle William didn't care. In a second, I'd be dead.

'Good! Shout for help. I've still got my story. Something was coming to get you . . . I shot at it, missed, and hit you instead.'

'But the Beast is dead,' I whispered.

At that moment, there was a low growl above me. Too close. I looked up, could see nothing for a moment, just a black, sleek movement silhouetted against the sky. The Beast.

Uncle William heard it too. His eyes moved from me . . . to the huge shape above. He stumbled back. There was terror in his eyes.

For the first time I saw it clearly. The snow falling on the fur of the great black Beast etched it white against the night sky. It had huge white fangs folded menacingly over its mouth, like some prehistoric sabre-toothed monster, like some beast from a nightmare. It would smell me. It must smell me in Jake's coat. It turned its eyes on me; those green eyes seemed to stare at me, singling me out. I had no breath to hold. I stared back, couldn't look away. The growl was low and deep in its throat, and as I stared I suddenly knew that I would rather die in the claws of the Beast than at the hands of Uncle William. But I didn't want to die at all.

And the Beast leapt.

'That was Kirsten's scream!' Her mother pulled at Faisal's dad. 'She's up there. She's in trouble.'

'Faisal will be with her. What are they doing here?'

'I don't know, but that was definitely her scream. Now, come on!'

At that second there was another scream. But this time it wasn't Kirsten.

Uncle William screamed. In that last second the Beast had turned its eyes on him and leapt. The gun went off. I saw sparks fly. Did the bullet hit the Beast? I couldn't tell. The Beast enveloped him, and he seemed to disappear, folded inside its fur. I stood frozen. Shaking. Didn't know what to do, where to go. Couldn't move. The Beast was huge; I'd never seen anything so huge. I saw Uncle William's face for a second, transfixed in terror. Then giant claws wrapped around his head and I saw a spurt of scarlet. Whose blood? Uncle William screamed again, held in the jaws of the Beast. They rolled together, in a tangle of black fur and blood, and suddenly, the mire was sucking them under. Uncle William was struggling wildly, screaming and yelling. And the Beast roared.

'I heard a shot!' Kirsten's mum screamed.

Faisal's dad had heard it too. It frightened him. Something else on the moors besides his son and Kirsten. Someone with a gun. But this was no time to panic. Their children needed them. He pulled at Kirsten's mother.

'You can show me the way through the swamp. We'll find them.'

58

The Dark Man heard the shot too, echoing through the fog. He heard the screaming – wild, terrified screaming, but not a boy's screams. A man's. He tried to take one more step. His foot sank again. He cursed the mire. The boy so close, almost in his grasp and he couldn't get to him.

There was a rattle at the door. Aunt Mary, sitting in her favourite armchair, jumped. She hadn't heard a car. She stood behind the door breathlessly. 'Who is it?' she called out.

There was no answer. She waited for a moment. Then, another rattle at the letterbox.

Couldn't be William, she was thinking. He had his key. Perhaps his car had broken down – and he had had to walk. He'd lost his key. Her hand shook as she reached out to pull aside the net curtain at the window.

At first she could see nothing. The fog was thick now, and the snow falling harder than ever. She moved closer to look. The fog seemed to shift, as if some wind had blown it clear, but there was no wind.

And there he was.

Noel.

Standing outside, under a tree, staring at her. Just standing. He was even smiling.

Mary let out a cry and fell back, collapsing on to an armchair.

No. It couldn't be. Noel was dead.

It was the other boy, trying to frighten her. He'd got away from William and had hurried back here to frighten her. Couldn't be Noel. Noel was dead.

Dead.

She stood up again, more sure of herself. She pulled the curtains aside.

And there was no one. He was gone . . . if he'd even been there in the first place. Her imagination. Had to be. She'd been through so much lately. No wonder her mind was playing tricks on her.

She peered closer. He was gone.

And suddenly his face rushed at her, zoomed out of the darkness, Close against the window. She fell back, screaming. It was Noel.

He grinned against the window. 'Aunt Mary . . .'

His voice, it was his voice. Singing her name like a song. 'Aunt Mary . . .'

She had fallen to the floor, hurt her head. She clutched at it as she crouched there, terrified.

'Aunt Mary . . .' His sing-song voice came drifting through the night.

She edged into a corner, waiting for any other sound.

It wasn't over yet. Shadows were looming closer. I braced myself for a fight. Was this the Dark Man? I prayed it was Kirsten, and even the police. Though what story I could tell them I didn't know.

'Ram, it's us!' The voice was barely a whisper. Faisal. I'd never been so glad to see anyone in my life. He was ready to run to me, but Kirsten held him back.

'The mire,' she said. 'It's all round you. You're right in the middle of it.'

'I know,' I said. 'Uncle William. The Beast . . .' My eyes were drawn to the murky swamp, I could still see them sinking, wrapped together now for eternity. I imagined them sinking further down, to hell, locked together, and it made me feel sick. I didn't have to explain. They knew what I meant.

'Stay where you are.' Kirsten swung her bike lamp around. I didn't move a muscle. Inside I was shaking with fear. 'What brought you here?'

'Your idea.' Faisal was trembling with enthusiasm and fear too. 'The Resistance. We helped Paul escape. We're going to help you too. My cousin's bringing his van . . . he'll be here soon. At your . . . I mean at Noel's house. We have to hurry.'

'You came all this way, followed me, to help me escape?'

'You have to escape, Ram. You've got a secret. It has to be a pretty big secret if this Dark Man's after you.'

'The Dark Man's here,' Kirsten said. I shuddered. I had known he would be.

'I have to get away.' I looked all around, trapped.

Kirsten fixed the light from her torch on the ground. 'There!' she said. 'If you look closely you can see a band of solid ground. My mum said they were like beams in a building. You walk across them; they guide you through the mire. Come here. I'll get you out.'

I tried to see, tried to make out anything solid. But there was nothing. 'It just looks like swamp.'

Kirsten called out, 'Trust me.'

I took one step, expecting to plunge down. Instead, my foot hit solid ground.

'There,' Kirsten said again, as if she was relieved too. 'And again.'

I was more confident with the next step, and with the next. My eyes never leaving the beam of the torch as it flickered shakily in Kirsten's nervous hands. But I was trusting her, not anything I could see. So close, yet still so far. I concentrated on trying to keep my balance. Hardly breathing.

'Now,' Kirsten said softly, 'step to the right, towards us.'

I could still make out nothing solid beneath my feet. 'You're sure?' I tried to sound brave, but I kept thinking of the Beast and Uncle William and the way they had been sucked under. Worse than drowning – way worse.

Kirsten didn't answer me. She was concentrating too hard, staring at the ground. 'Go,' she said, bossy as ever.

It was like a game of chess, one move after another, and I was the pawn.

At last, I was close enough to reach out and touch them. I felt like hugging them both. I grabbed at Faisal's jacket, gripped it tight.

'Come on,' Kirsten said. 'We're not out of the woods yet . . . or the mire.'

59

Aunt Mary crawled across the floor, afraid to look out-side. She'd heard no other sounds for so long she was beginning to think once again that her imagination had been playing tricks on her. Yet, she was still terrified.

Why was this happening to her? She hauled herself on to a seat and tried to think.

Noel was dead.

The other boy – well, William had probably dealt with him already. Or . . . a thought rose in her, a terrify-ing thought. She tried to put it down but it kept bubbling to the surface.

Was it William who'd been dealt with? And this boy was back here, pretending again to be the real Noel, just to terrorise her?

How could anyone be so cruel?

But it had been Noel's face she had seen outside the window. Noel.

She blinked, closed her eyes tightly trying to picture the boy, but it was Noel she kept seeing. His eyes, his face, his hair. She couldn't separate the two of them.

'William! Hurry back!' She needed him here. She was too afraid . . .

A scratching at the window, and then that voice again. 'Aunt Mary . . .'

That same sing-song voice, a whisper through the fog. She felt her heart tighten.

It came again. The scratching, like a skeleton's fingers against the glass.

'Aunt Mary . . .'

She leapt from her seat. Her teeth were chattering. She took one step, then another to the window, terrified to go too close. Even before she dared to open the curtains she could make him out, see his outline through the softly falling snow. She screamed. Couldn't take it any more.

'I'll get you! I'll get you!' She was hysterical, running for the front door, still screaming as she hauled it open.

And he was gone, as she knew he would be. There was no one there. Just falling snow and wisps of fog.

He wasn't real. He couldn't be real. All of this was in her mind. She ran into the yard, looked all around for him, threw open the door of the garage, expecting him to lunge at her. But the door only smacked against wood and slammed closed again. She had run all around the yard before she thought to look for his footprints, and by that time she had run so wildly in her fear, the only footprints she could see were her own.

She screamed into the night, 'Where are you?'

Was that a sound behind her?

She swivelled round but there was nothing. Of course there was nothing – just a ribbon of light from the open door.

Noel was dead. By this time, with any luck, the other

boy would be dead too.

She ran back to the house. She would bolt the door, tuck herself into a safe corner and wait. Wait till William came back.

Soon. He'd be back soon.

Until then, she would hide, with her hands clasped tightly round her ears to blot out any sounds. So she couldn't hear that voice from the grave call out . . . 'Aunt Mary.'

I followed Kirsten. She led us, holding her lamp high, lighting the path through the dark night.

I grabbed at her as I saw another silhouette in the fog. Someone was there in the distance, trapped, as I had been, in the swamp. The outline was so vague and yet I recognised it straight away, recognised the shape, the menace.

Faisal seemed to recognise it too. He grasped my arm. 'I've just realised who the black car belongs to.' He sounded relieved. 'I knew he'd come to help,' he whispered. 'It's OK, Ram. Everything's going to be OK now. It's Mr McGuffin.'

I gasped. McGuffin. The man who'd been staying with the Darlings. He'd been so close after all and I hadn't known. Now he was even closer. A few more steps and he would see me.

Faisal touched my arm. 'It's Mr McGuffin,' he said again.

'No, Faisal,' I warned him. 'It's the Dark Man.'

'I knew he was up to something,' Kirsten muttered.

'But he's Mr Darling's friend,' insisted Faisal.

'Didn't you know Mrs Darling takes in boarders?' Kirsten said. 'He was boarding with them.'

Faisal only took a moment to take it all in. 'He'll see us. He'll come after you. We have to do something.' He made a decision. 'Ram, give me your jacket.'

I plucked at Jake's coat. 'This?'

Faisal shook his head. 'No, the red jacket – the one you wore as Noel. It's underneath that coat, isn't it? Give that to me.'

'But why?' Even as I spoke I was pulling Jake's coat off me. And then the red jacket.

'He thought Noel was you, hiding in the garage. He ran after you as soon as he realised the mistake he made. If he was watching the house, then maybe he saw you going off with Uncle William.'

'Knew then that he'd been following the wrong boy, but he had still been led to the right place.' This was Kirsten.

'He's only seen you wearing the red jacket. If I wear this jacket and put the hood up,' Faisal said, 'he'll think it's you he's following.'

I suddenly stopped what I was doing. 'No, Faisal. You don't know how dangerous he is. He would kill you.'

Faisal began pulling the jacket from my fingers. 'He didn't hurt Noel. When he sees it's me and not you, he'll go off after you. He won't waste time with me. He's not interested in me.'

Kirsten spoke softly. 'It's a good idea, Faisal. If you keep going down there are no more bogs that way. The mire's up there.' She nodded to the hills. 'I know it, but he won't. You can run. Keep ahead of him. Keep going down, and you'll come to the road, lead him away from us, and I'll take Ram the other way, towards the bikes.'

I didn't want them to do it. It was too dangerous. But they wouldn't listen to me.

Faisal stood up straight. 'We're the Resistance,' he said boldly. 'I know where I'm going. Know this place like the back of my hand. Go, you've got to get away.'

'Are you sure?' I was afraid for him, afraid for us all.

'Of course I'm sure.'

'When I say run . . . go for it,' Kirsten whispered. And suddenly her voice was a wild shout. 'Run!'

There were three of them. He could make them out vaguely through the snow and fog. One of them had to be the boy. Yes. He recognised the jacket he'd been wearing in the car. Bright red in the snow. If only he could run. They were moving. They had seen him, recognised him too. He stepped forward, heard the girl call out, 'Run!' – and they did. The boy ran on alone – hero to the last.

The Dark Man began to move step by step through the mire. If there was no mire for them, there was none for him. His eyes never left the running boy. He was going down, heading for the road. He was too close not to take the chance. Mire or no mire, he would get him this time, surely.

Knew this place like the back of his hand? That was a

joke. Faisal could get lost in his own house. Faisal had never run so fast. Never had to. He was no athlete, but he was sure he could beat the Dark Man. Mr McGuffin! His hero. Yet, even as he ran, he wondered why he hadn't suspected him before. The way he had fought Wilkie, like a professional. How could he have learnt to fight like that? *Bet he's a hit man for the Mafia*, Faisal thought. *And the secret Ram knows is the name of the top man, the godfather.* Even the car he drove looked like a Mafia car. Sleek and black, just like him. The mystery of him, everything about him – sinister.

He heard him coming behind him, risking the mire to get to Ram. Faisal had to lead him away from Ram. Ram had to get away.

Kirsten's mother was still crying. Would she never stop crying! 'I know we're just missing them. They're here somewhere. I heard her scream. You heard it too, didn't you?' She was holding tight on to Faisal's dad's hand. It was almost painful, but he wouldn't let go. He was made of better stuff.

She called again, as she had been calling so often, 'Kirsten, can you hear me?'

Kirsten stopped. 'That's my mum! She's here looking for me.' She turned, looked back up into the dark moorland. She thinks I'm still there.'

'You go back, get her.'

Kirsten thought about it for only a second, shook her

head. 'No. You've got to get to the cottage. Abdullah's coming.' She looked back into the darkness. 'Mum will find Faisal. He'll be safe from the Dark Man.'

Another call rang out into the night. 'Faisal! Where are you?' This time calling for Faisal. His dad.

Kirsten smiled. 'He'll find him. His dad'll find him. Come on, grab a bike.'

I looked at the Dark Man's BMW. 'First,' I said, 'there's something I have to do.'

Faisal heard his dad calling. His dad was close by. He wanted so much to call out to him. 'I'm here!' But he still had to pretend he was Ram, had to keep running. He backed up against some rock, found there was nowhere else for him to go. The shadow of Mr McGuffin – why did he keep thinking of him as Mr McGuffin? – was looming ever closer.

'I've got you now.' Even his voice was sinister. He moved towards him, still sure he was closing in on Ram. So much hate in the voice. Why did he hate Ram so much? What was it Ram knew that was so important?

Faisal pulled the hood low over his face. He kept his head down, stepped further into the shadow of the rock.

The man reached for him, jerked Faisal towards him, and the hood fell back. Faisal's face was revealed. The man stepped back, angry, his face dark with rage. 'You!' he said.

He had Faisal's arm tight. Now he could see his eyes, dark eyes, with something in them that Faisal didn't understand at first. Then he realised what it was and

Faisal's legs gave way with terror. There was death in his eyes. Faisal's death. Why had he been so sure the man would simply throw Faisal aside and run after Ram? Now he was sure he would kill him first.

But Faisal still had one last chance. His dad was close by. Not a fighter, but at least he was here. He suddenly yelled so loudly his throat ached. 'Dad! Dad! I'm here! Help!'

Hear me, he prayed. *Please, hear me!*

60

We both heard Faisal's cry, faint in the distance, but full of terror. He was in trouble. 'I have to go back and help him,' I said, ready to run back.

Kirsten grabbed me. 'What good would it do? You wouldn't get there in time. My mother's there, and his dad's there.' Her voice was a sob. 'So you can't go back. It wouldn't do anybody any good.' And suddenly Kirsten was crying. 'He's so brave. I couldn't have done what he did. Oh please, God, let him be all right.'

And I knew if anything happened to Faisal I would never forgive myself either.

She looked at her watch, trying to stop from crying. 'Abdullah will be coming with the van. He won't wait for ever. We'd better hurry.' She took one last look up towards the dark moors from where Faisal's cry had come. 'He'll be OK. I know he will . . .'

Aunt Mary heard the knock at the door. She froze. He was back again. She pressed herself further into the corner. No more knocks, but she saw shadows passing the windows. Back and forth. He wasn't alone now. He had

272

brought someone else.

The other boy. They had both come back to get her.

She folded herself up as if she was back in her mother's womb. He mustn't see her. She would cower here and wait till he went away again. Till they both did.

She held her breath as a shadow came close to the window, seemed to peer inside. Could he get in? She imagined him melting through the glass, suddenly forming inside the room.

The thought made her sweat.

No. If she crouched here long enough, he'd leave. She'd hide here and pretend to be invisible and he would go away.

'Mrs Christie, will you open this door? I can see you there in the corner.'

She leapt to her feet, almost tumbling over the table.

'Mrs Christie, it's the police!'

The police? Why? What were they doing here?

'It's not bad news, Mrs Christie. Just a few questions. Nothing to worry about. But could you open the door, please?'

Not bad news? Then nothing had happened to William. She ran to the door, glad of company, human company. Real people.

There were two of them standing on the doorstep. The older one leant forwards and stared at her. 'Are you OK, Mrs Christie? You don't look well.'

She realised she must look dishevelled, worried. Perhaps even pale. She tried to compose herself. She was fine now. Someone else was here, and she would keep them here till William returned. Someone human and alive, even if it was the police.

'I'm fine.' Her voice came out like a squeak.

'May we come inside?'

She was even more glad of that. Someone solid, in her house. Two policemen filling her living room with common sense and normality. She moved aside to let them pass. She was more in control of herself now.

'What's this about?' she said.

'We've been informed that two of the pupils from the school, Faisal Yusaf and Kirsten Stewart, have gone missing. They're friendly with your nephew, Noel, who is the only other pupil in the school. The parents seem to think they came here at some point.'

Was that all? She couldn't keep the relief out of her voice. 'No. I haven't seen them at all. And I've been here all evening.'

'Maybe your nephew saw them,' the older man said. 'You know what children are like. They might have sneaked here, come in the back door, had some kind of secret assignation. Could we have a word with him?'

She swallowed, thinking fast. William had said they mustn't inform the police of Noel running away until he returned from the moors. 'He's asleep. Sound asleep. Been asleep for ages. He had a headache.' Hadn't she said that when the girl phoned earlier? Should she have told him the girl phoned? Too late now.

The policeman couldn't have been more polite. 'Would you mind waking him?'

'I don't really want to disturb him. It was a terrible headache. Couldn't it wait till morning?'

'I don't really think so. I'm afraid we must insist.

Children missing on the moors – can't take any chances, you know.'

Mustn't look guilty, she was thinking, trying to work out what to do. *If only William was here*. Should she tell them now that the boy had run away, that his uncle was out searching for him?

No. Too suspicious that she'd lied in the first place.

And it came to her. The perfect answer. She would go up to his room to wake him, find him gone. She would scream. Faint perhaps – always a good touch. 'His bed hasn't even been slept in,' she would yell. Couldn't work out better if she'd planned it that way, she thought.

She flashed him one of her famous smiles. 'Well, of course I'll wake him up, for the children's sake.'

She turned to go out of the living room, when, just at that moment, the door opened.

'What's happening, Aunt Mary? Why are the police here?'

He was rubbing his eyes as if he'd been disturbed in his sleep. He was wearing his pyjamas.

He was Noel.

And Aunt Mary began to scream.

61

'Where is he?' Mr McGuffin demanded. He had Faisal by the throat. He would strangle him if he had to. His life was nothing to him. He pulled the string of the hood tighter. 'Tell me where he went!'

Faisal saw his life flash before him, saw his mother's face. And his aunties' and his granny's. Even caught a glimpse of Kirsten's. Was this how he was meant to die? He wanted to have the strength to push him away, but something was ebbing from him. Was that his life?

Still he shook his head. He wouldn't tell. He knew no matter what this man did to him, he would never betray Ram. There was too much hate in this man's eyes. Ram's secret must be a powerful one.

'Take your hands off my son!'

The voice came from somewhere far away. Almost as if it was in a dream.

And there, in the last moments when he thought his life was over, came his dad, rushing through the night, through the fog, like an avenging angel. For a moment Faisal was sure he was seeing a ghost; that he had died indeed, and this was only the spectre of his father.

But he was real. He came so fast that Mr McGuffin

was taken totally by surprise. He let go of Faisal, stepped back, and his dad leapt on him, bringing him down. Faisal could breathe again. He fell to the ground, racked with coughs, and watched as the two men tumbled together, locked in combat. One of them, his dad. His dad! No wonder he thought it was a dream. His dad was fighting with Mr McGuffin. Faisal wanted to help, didn't know how to, or even if he had the strength to do anything.

Anyway, it seemed his dad didn't need him. He fought like a tiger, smaller than Mr McGuffin but tough like steel. He fought like a man who knew how to fight. Finally, the big dark man rolled away from him. He wanted the fight over, couldn't waste time here. He didn't care about winning, only catching up with Ram. He was on his feet in an instant. His eyes glanced towards Faisal, then back at his dad, already heading for him again, and suddenly, he was gone. One minute there, the next he had disappeared into the fog.

Faisal's dad hugged him. Mrs Stewart was becoming impatient. 'Why did Kirsten go off on her own?'

Faisal had never seen her so upset, would never have thought her capable of such tears. It was as if she really loved Kirsten. That came as a shock to Faisal. Kirsten's mother really did love her.

But the real shock was his dad. He still couldn't get over it. When he saw him racing through the fog to his rescue, saw him leap on Mr McGuffin, fight with him to save his son, he was so proud. 'Where did you learn to fight like that, Dad?' he asked him.

'I was not always an estate agent, Faisal. I was in the army once, you know. A soldier. Fought for Queen and country . . . or I would have done if there had been a war then.'

His dad's glasses were broken, his trousers ripped at the knees. His face was dirty. Faisal thought he'd never looked more handsome.

'Where is Kirsten?!' her mother asked again.

Faisal didn't know what to say, couldn't tell the truth, not till Ram was safe. He'd been sworn to secrecy. Ram had to get away. No one must know about Ram. That was the plan. The dilemma was solved for him. Kirsten's mother screamed, 'The Beast! We have to find Kirsten before she does.'

'The Beast is dead,' Faisal said. 'It went into the swamp.'

'And Kirsten? Where's Kirsten?'

'She's back at Noel's. She'll be waiting there for you.'

Kirsten's mum didn't need to know anything else. She turned. 'Come on. We have to hurry.'

'Be careful of the mire,' Faisal's dad said.

'I could get out here blindfolded,' she snapped, in that moment the old Mrs Stewart again and just like Kirsten.

🏃

More anger. The boy had let his tyres down! He kicked at the car, saw the bike tracks. Two bikes – the boy, probably the girl too. He was breathless with anger, shaking with it. Children fooling him this way once again. He looked at the other two cars on the track. The car belonging to Christie had no keys in it, he had checked

278

that earlier. But the other car, doors wide open, a rushed panic exit. Good chance the keys would be left inside. He hurried forward, smiled when he saw the keys swinging in the ignition. In a second he was in the front seat, and slammed the door shut. In another moment he was racing down the road.

We had reached Noel's house. The lights were on, a police car sat outside. Was Noel inside now, I wondered, taking his rightful place, scaring the wits out of Aunt Mary? I hoped so. Operation Ram successful. Further up the road, Abdullah's white van was tucked in behind some trees. You would miss it if you weren't looking for it. My escape.

Kirsten pulled me on. 'Come on.' She glanced up the dark road, watching for headlights. 'He'll be close behind us. He could be here at any time.'

'Will you be OK?'

'I've been thinking about my mum . . .' Kirsten said. 'I thought she had a boyfriend – that was why my dad left. But I don't think so now. I heard them fighting, and she was crying. And she shouted, "She's killed someone and it's all my fault." I didn't understand what she meant at the time, but I think now she was talking about the Beast. The Beast killed someone and it was all her fault. I think my mother and the research facility had something to do with the Beast, because all this started when she was first sighted.'

'Your mother cares about you, Kirsten. I think you know that now. She's out looking for you . . .'

'I know. I know she is.'

No more time. I had to go.

'How can I ever thank you, Kirsten? For doing all this for me.'

'Keep safe, find out what your secret is.' She was smiling, but all the time her eyes kept glancing up the road, watching. 'Please go, I couldn't bear it if you got this far and then he caught you. He's not the type to let flat tyres hold him back.'

I looked too, waiting for a car to burst through the fog, then I started heading for the van. I stopped suddenly and turned back to her. I was thinking fast. I always had to be one step ahead of the Dark Man. 'No,' I said. 'I don't want him to get me now.'

62

Kirsten's mother couldn't believe it. Her car was gone. 'He must have taken it! That man!'

'He must have,' Faisal said. He pointed to the BMW. 'Look, his tyres are flat.'

Faisal smiled at that. Good old Ram. Always one step ahead of the Dark Man.

'And no keys in this one!' Kirsten's mum kicked the car in anger.

And yet another surprise from Faisal's dad. 'No problem. Lucky this is an old car,' he said. 'I'll hot wire it.'

Kirsten had been right. Ram had only just gone when the car appeared, racing down the road. Her mother's car. At first she almost jumped in front of it, ready to wave, but it didn't even slow down at the driveway to Noel's house. She caught a glimpse of the face behind the wheel as the car shot past – a face taut with anger. She prayed the van could stay ahead of him. Abdullah knew the road so well, knew every twist and turn. She was sure he could stay ahead of him, and once on the dual carriageway, perhaps lose him completely. She prayed they had done the right thing. Ram couldn't get caught now.

She tried to compose herself as she headed for the cottage. The night wasn't over yet. Another part of Operation Noel to see through. The door of the cottage was pulled open as she neared it. A policeman stood there, looking grim. 'And what are you doing there, young lady?'

Kirsten stepped inside. 'I came to see Noel,' she said.

It was only ten minutes later that Faisal came running into the house. An excited Faisal. Kirsten beamed with pleasure when she saw him. She almost leapt on him. 'Faisal! You're OK!'

He grinned. 'Why? Were you worried about me? Bet you were.'

'Worried about you, bonehead? In your dreams.'

Fellow conspirators.

His father followed him into the house. Faisal thought he looked taller. Even with the torn trousers and the broken glasses he was beginning to look like an estate agent again. But never to Faisal.

His dad was glad to see the policemen there. 'Something terrible has happened –' he began. Didn't get to finish. Kirsten's mother came bursting in and as soon as she saw Kirsten she was in floods of tears again. *Boy*, Faisal thought, *she can certainly cry*. The ice maiden had melted. She grabbed at her daughter, hugged her so tightly Faisal was sure Kirsten's face went blue.

The policeman calmed them all down. 'Before we

begin to discuss anything else, there is a matter of identification.' He looked at Faisal. 'Young man,' he said, 'can you identify this boy as Noel Christie?'

The policeman touched Noel's shoulder. Noel was wearing pyjamas and tartan slippers. He looked totally at home here.

Faisal noticed for the first time the woman cowering in the corner, whimpering like a baby. Aunt Mary. He glanced from her, to Kirsten. Kirsten said at once. 'Well, of course he's Noel, I've already told you that. Who else could he be?'

The policeman looked annoyed at Kirsten. 'Let the boy answer, please.' He asked Faisal again. 'Is this Noel Christie?'

Faisal began to laugh. 'Is this a wind-up?' he asked. 'It's Noel. Of course, it's Noel.'

Aunt Mary leapt towards him, had to be held back by the other policeman. 'They're in it together! I hate them.'

'What do you mean, "Is this Noel Christie?"' Faisal's father asked. 'That is a very strange question to ask.'

Faisal was looking at his dad in a whole new way. He had found out so many things about him tonight. He could fight, and hot wire a car. He grinned at him.

'Can you identify him, sir?' the policeman asked.

Faisal held his breath. If he knew one thing about his dad that would never change, it was that he would never tell a lie. His father studied Noel. Suddenly, Faisal was glad his glasses were broken. 'Well, yes, he's the boy I saw at the school. Of course, I hardly saw him at all . . .'

The policeman turned to Kirsten's mother. 'And you,

madam. Can you say this is Noel Christie?'

She was still hugging Kirsten as if her daughter might run off at the first opportunity. Mrs Stewart merely glanced at Noel. 'There are much more serious issues here. I have important information about the research facility.'

'Madam, it's a simple question.'

She sighed. 'Of course the boy is Noel Christie.' Kirsten's mum had never really seen him either; just a glimpse, she had hardly looked at him. She was back to her old bossy self. The policeman recognised that at once. 'Besides I have important information about the research facility, and there was a man – he chased these children up on to the moors. Almost killed young Faisal here, and he stole my car.'

'Yes, madam. One thing at a time.' The policeman sounded harassed. Probably the limit of his policing up to now had been dealing with a traffic offence and giving out parking tickets, Faisal thought. All this was too much for one night.

They heard a car pull up outside. The policeman moved to the door. 'Ah, that'll be the teacher.'

Faisal gulped. Kirsten stiffened. The one blip in the whole plan. Mr Darling. 'I contacted him,' the policeman went on. 'If anyone can identify this boy, surely his teacher can.'

63

He could see the white van winding its way down the narrow road, had seen it snaking off as the girl had tried to stop him at the house. Did she think he was so stupid that he would stop for her? He would catch it. He put his foot down on the accelerator and the car speeded up. Did the van? He didn't think so, didn't think the van driver had seen him yet. The driver might even be oblivious to what was hiding in the back of the van.

He might have missed it too, if he hadn't recognised it as the same van that had visited the school. Perhaps it had come back to deliver some shopping and the boy had taken the opportunity to hide in the back. The Dark Man had spotted it turning quietly from the cover of the trees and on to the main road; turning almost as if it could slip into the night, unseen.

The boy was in the back. He was convinced of that. A daring little plan, but he would catch up soon. He would have him soon.

Mr Darling had brought his wife with him. Faisal had never seen him look so dishevelled. There was an ugly bruise on his cheek, yellow from the fight he'd had with Wilkie. His collar was sticking up from his overcoat and it was all buttoned up wrong, as if he'd been lying in an armchair, relaxing, and as soon as he'd received the phone call he'd left in a hurry.

Mrs Darling came behind him, clutching his hand. Faisal almost wished he could clutch Kirsten's hand. Boy, he was in a bad way thinking like that.

'What's this all about?' Mr Darling asked. He saw Kirsten and Faisal. 'Thank goodness, they're safe and sound.'

'A great deal to tell you about that, Mr Darling,' Faisal's dad said.

The policeman said, 'All we need from you for the moment, sir, is for you to identify one of these children.'

Mr Darling's eyes flashed surprise, shock even, and he smiled. 'Identify one of these?' His eyes went from Kirsten to Faisal.

The policeman moved aside. Now he could see Noel. He stared at him. Faisal glanced at Kirsten. She looked nervous, but being Kirsten she stepped forward. 'No wonder you look surprised, sir. They're asking us if this is really Noel Christie.' She hauled Noel towards her. 'I mean, sir, who else could it be?'

Aunt Mary staggered to her feet unsteadily. As if she was drunk. 'No. He's not Noel! You don't understand.'

Noel looked at the teacher. 'She scares me, sir,' he said.

Faisal spoke now. 'Who else could he be, but Noel? What's going on, sir?'

The policeman said again, 'I'm sorry we have to ask

this, sir, but can you identify this boy as Noel Christie?'

They all stared at him now. Faisal pleaded silently. *Please, sir, it's up to you!*

It was Noel who broke the silence. He took something from the pocket of his dressing gown, handed it to the teacher. It was a photograph. 'I mean, sir. Who else can I be? There I am in the photograph. It's at my cousin's wedding. I'm there with Aunt Mary and Uncle William. My name's on the back. Look.' He turned the photograph around, let him see. Pointed to his name, Noel. 'Who else could I be but the real Noel Christie?'

Aunt Mary let out a strangled scream, lunged at Noel. The younger policeman held her back. Noel stepped closer to Mrs Darling. She slipped an arm around his shoulders, pulled him towards her.

'I'm scared of her, sir,' he said again.

Mr Darling still studied the photograph. He looked back at Noel. Then at Aunt Mary.

'He's dead, I'm telling you. Dead! That's not him!' She was shaking, staring at Noel with such venom in her eyes no one could miss it. Everything was in the teacher's hands. They all waited for his answer.

He took a deep breath. 'I don't understand what all this is about. But . . .' He looked at his wife, her arm around the boy's shoulders. He gripped the photo tightly between his fingers, held it out to the policeman. 'Of course this is the real Noel Christie. Who else could it be?'

Aunt Mary screamed, 'No!'

64

The Dark Man caught up with the van, pulled in front of it on the narrow road. Nowhere for it to go. Nothing for it to do but stop. He jumped from the car, hauled open the front door. A dim-looking Asian boy sat in the front, listening to music. His eyes widened with alarm when he saw him.

'What's the problem, pal? You want the van, you take it.' He held his hands up high as if he was being robbed. There was no one else in the front, just the idiot boy. He had no time to waste on him. He ran to the back. He could see it all now, the whole plan. The van would take him to safety. He hauled open the doors, leapt into the back. Already he could hear the driver jumping out of the van, pounding down the road to the dual carriage-way. The Dark Man pulled a penlight torch from his pocket. He could imagine the boy cowering in the back, behind boxes, afraid. Knowing it was over at last. He'd been caught. He pulled boxes, scattered sweets and crisps everywhere.

And he wasn't here.

There was no one here. He'd been fooled again.

I moved on. Getting as far away as possible. I had taken a chance, but I was sure he would think I had gone in the van, follow it, soon catch up with it, find out I wasn't hiding inside. But at least it would give me time, much needed time to get away from him, moving as fast as I could. All the time I was thinking of what Kirsten had said.

She.

Kirsten said her mother had called the Beast 'she'.

The Beast was female.

And I remembered the night I saw her, carrying a full-grown sheep in her mouth, not eating it where she hunted, but taking it somewhere else. She hadn't been interested in me. She had more important things on her mind. She had a family to feed.

The Beast had cubs.

The cubs had waited for their mother's return. It seemed now she would never come. They were alone.

But she had done well.

She had already taught them to hunt.

Noel was going home with the Darlings, just for the night, for the time being at least. 'We'll look after him,' Mr Darling had said. Noel seemed happy with the arrangement.

Mrs Darling took his hand. 'Come on, then, Noel.

You must be tired.'

Aunt Mary was taken away in an ambulance. Faisal had been waiting for the men in white coats to rush in and put her in a straitjacket, then carry her, screaming, outside. He was most disappointed when, not only were they both middle-aged ladies in nurses' outfits, but they led her out very gently and by this time Aunt Mary just looked vacant.

'What would we have done if Mr Darling had said it wasn't Noel?' Faisal whispered to Kirsten as they watched her go.

'I never had any doubts. You said it yourself, he's a good man. He saw the photograph. The photograph was of the real Noel. He must have figured out that there had been something very fishy going on.'

'It's been an exciting night,' Faisal said. 'I'm going to be really bored after this.'

'I don't intend to be bored ever again,' Kirsten said.

'What do you mean by that?'

She smiled. 'There must be other children on the run who need help. We could find them.'

'You mean keep the Resistance going?'

'Yeah. Ram was right. It's a good idea. We used it once, why can't we use it again?'

Faisal thought about it. 'Me and you, a team, Kirsten. Who would have thought it?'

'You and I are not a team, bonehead. I'm the boss and don't you forget it!'

'In your dreams, Kirsten.'

Just then his dad came back into the house. 'Faisal, someone's stolen your bike!'

I was long gone. On Faisal's bike. I'd leave it somewhere, then I'd carry on. I'd try to find out the truth. I'd been looking in all the wrong places. I knew that now. Looking among the missing. I should have been looking among the dead. I was dead, the Dark Man had told me the first time we'd come face to face in the liftshaft, now I understood. Like Noel, everyone thought I was dead. That was why no one was looking for me. And what was the proof I had? What was the secret? Was Faisal right? Could it be on the scale of Operation Overlord? How could I find a way into my memory? There had to be something that would bring it all back to me.

I would find out the truth eventually.

I'd escaped the Dark Man again.

I was meant to live.

'Then, I heard it: a noise along the dark corridor.
I couldn't make out what the noise was, couldn't
see a thing, but something was up there in the
darkness. Something that seemed to glow green.
Something swishing rhythmically toward me out
of the blackness.

Ever had that feeling of terror when you can't
see what's coming, but you know it might be
your worst nightmare?'

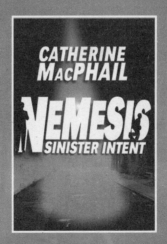

CATHERINE
MacPHAIL

NEMESIS
SINISTER INTENT

*The third instalment in MacPhail's
thrilling Nemesis series*
COMING SOON